SCHOOL

'A wholly original presence in modern literature'
ANDREW MOTION

'Delightful, laced with wry and witty observations'
DAILY MAIL

'She has a receptive and wholly distinctive genius'
A. N. WILSON

'Has one of the funniest opening pages Spark has ever written and it's full of her incomparable humour'
EVENING STANDARD

'I consider Muriel Spark to be the most gifted and innovative British novelist of her generation'
DAVID LODGE

'Spark is a natural, a paradigm of that rare sort of artist from whom work of the highest quality flows as elementally as current through a circuit'
NEW YORKER

'A profoundly serious comic writer whose wit advances, never undermines or diminishes, her ideas'
NEW YORK TIMES BOOK REVIEW

Muriel
Spark

The FINISHING
SCHOOL

CANONGATE
Edinburgh · London

This Canons edition published in 2016 by Canongate Books Ltd,
14 High Street, Edinburgh EH1 1TE

www.canongate.tv

First published in Great Britain in 2004 by Penguin Books Ltd,
80 Strand, London WC2R 0RL

2

British Library Cataloguing-in-Publication Data
A catalogue record for this book is available on
request from the British Library

ISBN 978 1 78211 757 5

Typeset in Sabon MT by Canongate Books Ltd

Printed and bound in Great Britain by Clays Ltd, St Ives plc.

I

'YOU BEGIN,' he said, 'by setting your scene. You have to *see* your scene, either in reality or in imagination. For instance, from here you can see across the lake. But on a day like this you can't see across the lake, it's too misty. You can't see the other side.' Rowland took off his reading glasses to stare at his creative writing class whose parents' money was being thus spent: two boys and three girls around sixteen to seventeen years of age, some more, some a little less. 'So,' he said, 'you must just write, when you set your scene, "the other side of the lake was hidden in mist." Or if you want to exercise imagination, on a day like to-day, you can write, "The other side of the lake was just visible." But as you are *setting* the scene, don't make any emphasis as yet. It's too soon, for instance, for you to write, "The other side of the lake was hidden in the fucking mist." That will come later. You are setting your scene. You don't want to make a point as yet.'

*

College Sunrise had begun in Brussels, a finishing school for both sexes and mixed nationalities. It was founded by Rowland Mahler, assisted by his wife, Nina Parker.

The school had flourished on ten pupils aged sixteen and upwards, but in spite of this flourishing, mainly by reputation,

1

Rowland had barely been able to square the books at the end of the first year. So he moved the school to Vienna, increased the fees, wrote to the parents that he and Nina were making an exciting experiment: College Sunrise was to be a mobile school which would move somewhere new every year.

They had moved, leaving commendably few debts behind, from Vienna to Lausanne the next year. At present they had nine students at College Sunrise at Ouchy on the lake. Rowland had just taken the very popular class, attended by five of the students, on creative writing. Rowland was now twenty-nine, Nina twenty-six. Rowland himself hoped to be a published novelist one day. To conserve his literary strength, as he put it, he left nearly all the office work to Nina who spoke good French and was dealing with the bureaucratic side of the school and with the parents, employing a kind of impressive carelessness. She tended to crush any demands for full explanations on the part of the parents. This attitude, strangely enough, generally made them feel they were getting good money's worth. And she had always obtained a tentative licence to run the school, which could be stretched to last over the months before they would move on again.

It was early July, but not summery. The sky bulged, pregnant with water. The lake had been invisible under the mist for some days.

Rowland looked out of the wide window of the room where he taught, and saw three of the pupils who had just attended his class, leaving the house, disappearing into the mist. Those three were Chris Wiley, Lionel Haas and Pansy Leghorn (known as Leg).

Chris: Seventeen, a student at College Sunrise at his own request. 'I can do university later.' And now? 'I want to write my novel. It struck me that College Sunrise was ideal for that.' Rowland remembered that first interview with red-haired

Chris with his mother and uncle. There was no father visible. They seemed to be well-off and perfectly persuaded to Chris's point of view. Rowland took him on. He had always, so far, taken everyone on who applied for entrance to College Sunrise, the result of which policy helped to give the school an experimental and tolerant tone.

But we come back to Chris as he and his two friends were watched from the window by Rowland: of all the pupils Chris caused Rowland the most disquiet. He was writing a novel, yes. Rowland, too, was writing a novel, and he wasn't going to say how good he thought Chris was. A faint twinge of that jealousy which was to mastermind Rowland's coming months, growing in intensity small hour by hour, seized Rowland as he looked. What was Chris talking about to the two others? Was he discussing the lesson he had just left? Rowland wanted greatly to enter Chris's mind. He was ostensibly a close warm friend of Chris – and in a way it was a true friendship – Where did Chris get his talent? He was self-assured. 'You know, Chris,' Rowland had said, 'I don't think you're on the right lines. You might scrap it and start again.'

'When it's finished,' said Chris, 'I could scrap it and start again. Not before I've finished the novel, though.'

'Why?' said Rowland.

'I want to see what I write.'

Nina, Rowland's wife and colleague, sat at a big round table in the general living room of College Sunrise. Round the table were five other girls, Opal, Mary, Lisa, Joan and Pallas.

'Where's Tilly?' said Nina.

'She's gone into the town,' said Opal. Tilly was known and registered at the school as Princess Tilly, but no-one knew where she was Princess of. She seldom turned up for lessons,

3

so Nina did not pursue the matter further. The subject was Etiquette or as Nina put it, '*Comme il faut.*'

'When you finish at College Sunrise you should be really and truly finished,' Nina told the girls. 'Like the finish on a rare piece of furniture. Your jumped-up parents (may God preserve their bank accounts) will want to see something for their money. Listen: when you eat asparagus in England, as everyone knows, you take it in your fingers, but the secret of exquisite manners with regard to asparagus is to eat it held in your left hand. Got it?'

'My parents are not jumped-up,' said Pallas. 'My father, Mr Kapelas, is of an old family of merchants. But my mother is ignorant. She wears expensive clothes, though.'

'Do they hang well on her?' said Mary, a blue-frocked, blue-eyed, fair English woman in the making. Her ambition was to open a village shop and sell ceramics and transparent scarves. 'Everything,' said Mary, 'depends on the hang. You see women with lovely clothes, but they don't hang right on them.'

'You are so right,' said Nina, which made Mary adore the teacher even more. Hardly anyone ever told Mary she was so right about anything.

'Well now,' said Nina, 'if you are offered a plover's egg as a snack, that, too, is taken with the left hand. I read about this in a manners' book, perhaps it was a joke; anyway, I can see that if you want your right hand to be free to shake someone else's hand, your left hand should hold the plover's egg, preferably, I suppose, between the folds of a tiny paper napkin. This is what your parents are paying for you to know, remember.'

'What's a plover?' said Pallas.

'Oh just a bird, there are lots of different species.'

'I like seagulls,' Pallas said.

'Do they make you homesick?' said Nina.

'Yes. All the sea things make me nostalgic for Greece.'

Opal said, 'We were to have gone to Greece for next spring if the crash hadn't happened in our family.' The crash was a bankruptcy which had left Opal's parents in ruin and distress, with which they were at present trying to cope. Opal's father would perhaps go to prison, so steeply had the family affairs crashed. Nina and Rowland had immediately offered to keep Opal on at the school without paying any fees for her lessons or her keep, a gesture which was greatly approved by the school at large.

'At large …' It was not in any sense a large school. College Sunrise could not in any way compete with the famous schools and finishing establishments recommended by Gabbitas, Thring and Wingate in shiny coloured brochures. Indeed, College Sunrise was almost unknown in the more distinctive educational circles, and in cases where it was known, it was frequently dismissed as being rather shady. The fact that it moved house from time to time, that it seldom offered a tennis court and that its various swimming pools looked greasy, were the subject of gossip when the subject arose, but it was known that there had so far been no sexual scandals and that it was an advanced sort of school, bohemian, artistic, tolerant. What they smoked or sniffed was little different from the drug-taking habits of any other school, whether it be housed in Lausanne or in a street in Wakefield.

With a total of eight paying students Nina and Rowland could just manage to cope and make a small profit. They employed a maid and a cook, a French teacher who was also Rowland's secretary, and a good-looking gardener and odd-job boy. Both Nina and Rowland aimed principally at affording Rowland the time and space and other opportunities to complete his novel, while passing their lives pleasantly. They in fact loved the school.

But the whole point of the enterprise was decidedly Rowland's novel. Nina believed in it, and in Rowland as a novelist, as much as he did himself.

Chris, as he walked with his two companions was thinking of the letter Rowland had sent to his uncle recommending specially the creative writing class at College Sunrise: 'This year's literary seminar pulls no punches investigating ideas of power and literature.' Chris was fascinated by this announcement. It would not leave his mind. He had heard it before – where did it come from? Suddenly, as he was gazing into the impenetrable sheet of mist on the lake, a ray of light swung across his memory: it was the phrase used to advertise an English literary festival. In his extraordinary mind Chris remembered the brochure precisely. He felt affectionate towards Rowland, almost protective. His own sense of security was so strong as to be unnoticeable. He knew himself. He felt his talent. It was all a question of time and exercise. Because he was himself unusual, Chris perceived everyone else to be so. He could not think of people as masses except when the question of organizing society arose, and that, thought Chris, should be a far simpler affair than the organizers made out. Left to themselves, people would arrange themselves in harmony. So he should be left alone to pursue ... well, anything. It was a good theory. In the meantime he found his tutor, Rowland, greatly amusing. Rowland had read the two opening chapters of the novel Chris was determined to write during his terms at College Sunrise. On his second reading: 'But this is quite good,' Rowland had whispered, as if speechless with amazement. Chris remembered every slightest phrase of that reaction. Rowland had read it over. 'Are you sure,' he said then, 'that you want to go on with this, or would you rather ...'

'Rather what?' Rowland did not continue that line of thought. 'The dialogue,' he said, 'how did you know about dialogue?'

'Oh, I've always read a lot.'

'Oh, you read a lot, I see. For an historical novel you have to ... And what, how ... Do you intend to finish it?'

'Oh, fully.'

'What is the story? How does it develop? Historical novels – they have to develop. How ... ?'

'No idea, Rowland. I can't foresee the future. All I know is the story will happen.'

'And you find our creative writing classes a help, of course ...'

'They're beside the point, in fact, but quite useful in many other respects.'

Rowland was frightened; he felt again that stab of jealous envy, envious jealousy that he had already experienced, on touching and reading Chris's typescript.

II

THE NOVEL CHRIS was writing was further advanced in his mind than he had conveyed to Rowland. A self-protective urge mixed with a desire to gain as much as possible from the creative writing class made him adopt the pose of a fairly blank set of intentions. In fact he had a plot settled in his mind.

The subject of his story was Mary Queen of Scots, beheaded in 1587 for scheming against the life of Elizabeth I of England. She was also accused of the murder of her husband Lord Darnley, twenty years before. Many since then had believed her guilty, many innocent. There were arguments both ways, one faction claiming that Mary and some of her noble followers were party to the murder, the other holding that she was innocent: the crime had been organized by rebellious noblemen, Mary's enemies.

Chris had a third proposition, and the pith of it was this: He went back to the day when a group of Scottish noblemen, led by Darnley, broke into her room at Holyrood where she was playing cards. They murdered with their daggers David Rizzio, her secretary, musician and close friend, of whom Darnley had become exceedingly jealous. Rizzio was Italian, gifted, ambitious. His family came from Turin.

According to Chris's novel, the murder of Darnley was arranged by Rizzio's family as an act of revenge. David Rizzio had brought to the Queen's court in Edinburgh, his younger brother Jacopo who was at the centre of the plot.

Chris didn't trouble to believe this theory one way or another, but he felt it would make a good story. It was to be an excitingly written novel, in addition to its originality. It was to be popular.

Leaving aside the story, of which Rowland was at present unaware, he had scrutinized the first fifteen pages of Chris's book at the same time as he experienced a choking sensation. No, no, this could not be, this is good, very expert. It can't be Chris's work – the logic doesn't hold that he could set such a scene. Something will have to go wrong. Root it out, stop it. And 'Oh, my God,' thought Rowland, 'what am I thinking?'

Chris came down to Ouchy from the town past a row of private villas, so quiet inside their gates, you would think that no-one was there.

It was the fourth house in the long road that he approached with expectation. The house stood behind a long low wall. Four times, now, at varying hours, he had passed this house, and – listen – the sound of a violin the moment he appeared passing the wall, and continuing till he had passed, when the music stopped. Once he had caught sight, only a flash, of a head and shoulder at an upper window. He could not tell whether it was a man or woman, or what age the person was. It was simply that someone watched for him to pass and played a few bars of an unknown tune on the violin and then, when he had reached the end of the wall, abruptly stopped.

It was getting dark. As he entered the hall of College Sunrise he heard, from Rowland's television, the familiar voice of Hazel on Sky News: 'As we go through this evening and into tonight ...' The weather in England was warm, scattered showers in the southeast and rain in the north of Scotland.

Chris tried to recall the few notes of the tune that was played on the violin, but the more he tried the more it escaped him. He decided to continue passing the house every day until he had resolved the question that arose. He went in search of Rowland, to tell him of the strange experience. 'Someone,' he said to Rowland, 'who has time to sit waiting for hours at the window.'

Rowland had turned down the television sound.

'Sit down,' he said.

'No, I've got to get on with my novel.'

'Oh, God, you'll wear yourself out. Take a night off.'

III

THE NEXT NIGHT about nine o'clock Rowland and Chris went along to the mysterious house of the violin. They found the gate open, the vestibule light on but the front of the house in darkness. On the front door was a well-shined brass plate: 'Dr Israel Brown'. Round the back of the house, which they approached carefully in the dark, there was equally no sign of an inhabitant. But a torchlight shone in the darkness on the pathway to the back door and French window. A man shaped himself forth, holding the torch. He was elderly and walked with a stoop, evidently a guardian or gardener of the house. 'Looking for someone?' he said in his sing-song Vaudois.

'We come from College Sunrise,' said Rowland. 'I understand there is a violin player in this house. I am looking for a violin teacher.'

The man laughed. 'Giovanna plays the violin,' he said. 'She doesn't need a job.'

'Who is Giovanna?' said Chris.

'Giovanna Brown, Dr Brown's aunt, believe it or not, although she is ten years his junior. It's one of those things that occur sometimes in families.'

'I believe I heard her play,' said Chris. 'I happened to be passing. A couple of times.'

'Ah.'

'Are they away?' said Rowland.

'Yes, they've left. If you want to leave a message there's a maid comes in the mornings.'

'No message,' said Rowland, 'just a courtesy call.'

Chris said, on the way back, 'Obviously she's a cripple or had an accident which induced her to sit at the window all day, so she played a joke on me when I passed by the house.'

'How you *romance* about things.'

'No, it's a perfectly logical supposition.'

Which it was, for the young aunt of Israel Brown had suffered a broken shin at an ice-hockey stadium in Vienna where she was studying music. She had been flown to her nephew's house at Lausanne to recover. Sure enough, she had amused herself by playing a few bars on her violin at the window where she sat daily with her leg up, as Chris, a red-haired target, was passing.

Neither Chris nor Rowland, however, were yet aware of this actual construction of events. Rowland said, 'Have you been taking anything?'

'No,' said Chris. 'I don't smoke or sniff while I'm writing. In fact, practically never.'

The choking sensation attacked Rowland again. 'I think you're working too hard and too long hours on that novel. Why don't you talk to Nina. She's very helpful.'

'I know.' Chris added, 'I didn't imagine the violin.'

'But if you did,' said Rowland, 'it wouldn't be your fault.'

Chris laughed. Then he said, 'Rowland, you don't like my novel, but I'm going to write it.'

They had reached College Sunrise and let themselves in. Pallas Kapelas, tall and swarthy and striking, was in the hall.

'My father,' she said, 'has lost his cards.'

'What cards?' said Rowland.

George Kapelas, Pallas's father, had recently stayed overnight at College Sunrise.

'His card index. He belongs to the card index generation. I have to send him my address book. I'll get it back.'

Chris started up the stairs to his room. Pallas followed. She looked over her shoulder. Rowland was watching them – why? Not really intending to wave a red rag in front of a bull, she called down, as she mounted, 'Getting on with your novel, Rowland?' All the students of Sunrise knew that he struggled with a novel. They often volunteered to give him ideas for it; which he accepted politely enough. They begged him to read it aloud to them, but the truth was, the book was not yet in any readable condition. It consisted of paragraphs here and there on his computer, changing from day to day. He was in a muddle, which was not to say he would not eventually get out of it, as in fact he was to do by writing a different sort of book.

Rowland, late that night, got out of bed. Nina woke. But he didn't make for the bathroom as Nina expected. He was now at the door of the bedroom. 'Where are you off to?'

'I don't know if I locked up –'

'Of course you did. I saw you.'

He went, all the same. Along the passage was the study, the floor piled high with the evidence of nine students, in several subjects of their daily exercises, which eventually he would catch up with. On his desk stood a computer. He sat at the desk and typed, 'The girl at the window. Her broken leg. Her violin. Her attraction to the Boy who Passes. She plays a tune. (A "little phrase" – Proust?) He stops, stares up at the house. Who is the player?'

Rowland felt he could start from there and lead into what he had written already about the callow teenager who felt he could write a novel, himself.

Nina had said, the other day, 'If Chris and his novel get on your nerves you know we can always send him home.

We could say he was neglecting his studies for the book he's writing.'

'They know he's writing a novel.'

'Yes, but it could unsettle the others who have to show some interest in the curriculum.'

'I don't want to part with Chris.'

'Neither do I. Not at all. But he bothers you, I've noticed.'

'You notice too much.'

IV

ROWLAND WAS SENDING his students under the care of
Elaine Valette, his secretary and the school's French teacher,
on a visit to the Château de Chillon, celebrated in Byron's
poem *The Prisoner of Chillon*. Under Rowland's tutelage
they had been studying the legend celebrated in the poem,
comparing it with the more sober but still exhilarating
history of the sixteenth century Genevan patriot François
Bonivard. Geneva was overcome by the Duke of Savoy and in
1530 Bonivard was imprisoned in a dungeon of the Castle of
Chillon standing, as it does, on the very verge of Lake Léman.

The Sunrise group comprised eight, the ninth, Princess
Tilly, having a pain in her stomach and so forced to lie on a
sofa for some hours, on this her bad day of the month.

It was a good day for all the rest. Rowland had promised
to accompany them on the trip but changed his plan at the
last minute. He had 'things on his desk' to attend to. Elaine
Valette was quite capable of looking after them.

'Don't forget to think of Bonivard,' he had told them that
morning. 'When you see the room where he lived for six years,
even although Byron's poem elaborates the historical facts,
it certainly does suggest the feelings and sensations of the
prisoner in that damp, dark dungeon, most of those years in
chains.' Rowland quoted the final stanza of Byron's account,
remarking that it revealed a strangely modern psychology:

At last men came to set me free;
    I ask'd not why, and reck'd not where;
It was at length the same to me,
Fetter'd or fetterless to be,
    I learn'd to love despair.
And thus when they appear'd at last,
And all my bonds aside were cast,
These heavy walls to me had grown
A hermitage – and all my own!
And half I felt as they were come
To tear me from a second home:
With spiders I had friendship made,
And watch'd them in their sullen trade,
Had seen the mice by moonlight play,
And why should I feel less than they?
We were all inmates of one place,
And I, the monarch of each race,
Had power to kill – yet, strange to tell!
In quiet we had learn'd to dwell;
My very chains and I grew friends,
So much a long communion tends
To make us what we are:– even I
Regain'd my freedom with a sigh.

They were to take the lake boat leaving Ouchy at 12.30, arriving at Chillon at 2 p.m. Célestine, Elaine's sister who had taken a temporary job with the school as its cook had been allowed to join them. She had made up a picnic lunch which Célestine carried in a basket.

'Why,' demanded Rowland of Chris, 'are you taking your back-pack?' (Chris called it his *zaino*. It was bulky and he wore it most of the time.)

'Force of habit. I might need something, a book or something …'

'Oh Chris, for God's sake leave it behind,' said Rowland; and it was the voiced opinion that Chris's cumbersome luggage would only bump into the other passengers and generally cause obstruction.

Chris took his money-card out of the *zaino* which he then handed to Nina; she had come to the porch to wave them goodbye. 'I'll put it in your room,' Nina said. They were to return on the boat leaving Chillon at about four-twenty, arriving at Ouchy at ten past six that evening.

'Wonderful getting rid of them for the whole afternoon,' Nina said.

It was three in the afternoon after lunch, which, in the cook's absence, Nina had prepared, and when the dishes had been washed up and Nina lay down for her nap, Rowland went to Chris's room. Nina had put Chris's bulging back-pack on a chair. Rowland heaved it on to the desk and opened it. He started to take out the contents one by one:

A 'marine blue' pullover, labelled *Peter Polo*
A grey T-shirt labelled *Celio*
A pair of blue and white trainer shoes, *Nike*

Rowland halted in his search and went to look into Chris's hanging cupboard. Yes, there were some clothes there, but still plenty of room. Why did Chris carry all these clothes about with him? He went back to the gaping back-pack. A pair of jeans, *Levi's*. A pair of white tennis socks. The label of the back-pack itself now came into view *East Pact*. Then came a watch *Sport Adidas*, a video of cars and tennis. There seemed no end to the contents. Rowland emptied the bag on to the bed – what a pile – What he was looking for were notes and books connected with Chris's novel. Where were they? He flicked through the notebooks; they were all school stuff. Nothing to do with Mary Stuart of Scotland and her sinister crew of courtiers. Rowland rummaged among the pile. Suspicious of everything, he didn't altogether know why, Rowland lifted the items one by one. Mostly French stuff ... Chris had evidently been in France recently. He did think, of course, that sooner or later he would come across a joint of some sort or some small pellets containing crack cocaine; that would be a find. But even more than dope, there was some secret of Chris's that Rowland wanted to get hold of. He was in a choking, suspicious frenzy about it. Chris wrote like a professional. How did he manage language so wonderfully at his age, and with so little experience? How? Rowland lifted the next items. A letter from his uncle, 'Hope you are all right. Keep at it. Anything you need, ring Winkler at the bank. Mary's going to Cowes ...'

Rowland picked up, next, a discman, *Sony*; punk music, Phil Collins, Michael Jackson, Coltrane. Telephone card 100 euros, a silk wallet marked *Quicksilver* containing a credit card *Crédit Lyonnais*, a key-ring marked *Quicksilver* holding three keys which Rowland smelt. Then a portable phone *Nokia* – *forfait* four hours in Swiss francs. The information on the phone showed nil.

Rowland made a neat pile of the examined material and continued with the considerable stuff that remained. Oh, yes, some of those *petite feuille* as they loved to call them – little papers to roll up their bac to smoke. A copy of *Fluide Glaciale* – the young people's old, awful, magazine. Not finished yet. No, not by a long way. Why do they carry all this about with them? A pearl necklace, a French/English dictionary, a Roget's Thesaurus, a *Levis's* fob-watch fixed on a belt, a Bob Marley disc, a block of writing-paper, a packet of condoms, unopened. Does he use Viagra, Rowland wondered, wildly searching, feverishly. Apparently no. There came next a very pale blue T-shirt with a picture of College Sunrise – a part of the school hand-out; two green apples.

When eventually he had finished he tried to get the lot back into the bag. He did it very neatly, and failed. There was simply no room. So he emptied the bag again and stuffed in the goods teen-age style. This time he was lucky. It would be obvious to Chris, he supposed, that his back-pack had been searched. Chris was not the sort to make a fuss. That was what was so disconcerting about Chris. He cared, really for nothing but that bloody book of his *Who Killed Darnley?* or whatever its title was to be. And anyway where was the latest part of the book? Where did he keep his work, his pages, his print-outs and his notes when he wasn't in the room? Who was keeping his computer? – it wasn't here. Rowland did up the last strap of the rucksack and turned to the desk. What was in the two desk drawers, one on top of the other on the right side of the desk? He caught a glimpse of someone standing in the doorway. It was Princess Tilly, tall, silent, dark-eyed.

'Tilly, how long have you been there?'

'Quite a time.'

'Spying?'

'Watching. What is there to spy?'

'I'm looking for Chris's book, the one he's writing.'

'It's with Pallas. She locks it up. She has his p.c.'

'Is that necessary? We don't need locks in this school.'

'Well we don't all want our things looked into.'

'Yes, I know. Look Tilly we've been good to you haven't we?'

'Don't worry. I won't tell Chris you've been searching through his stuff.'

Meanwhile Chris, on his way back with the others from the grim castle of Chillon to catch the evening boat, was thinking only of the sixteenth century, and the hardiness of Bonivard who died in 1570 four years after the death of Rizzio. They might have met. They lived in different worlds yet it was not impossible that the lordly Savoyard should encounter the young Piedmontese diplomat who won his way into the courts of Europe.

V

TILLY MET HER fellow students at the porch doorway of
College Sunrise when they returned from their trip to Chillon.

As they entered, Tilly said, 'Rowland went into Chris's
room after Claire had finished cleaning. He emptied Chris's
zaino and I peeped round the door. I can be so silent, oh, you
wouldn't know how silent. But Rowland saw me. I promised
not to tell. Rowland examined everything closely and put it
back. We had a filthy lunch.'

Chris laughed lightly. He said, 'He wants my secrets.
However, I like Rowland. I couldn't manage without him in
a way. He's the yolk of an egg. The white part's not enough.
The yolk, for better or for worse …'

'Do you know what he said? He said "Tilly" he said
"We've been good to you haven't we, Tilly?" Oh yes, you
have, I said. Don't worry, I won't say a word. I thought he
was going to make advances at me.'

'You mean "*to*" you. Well, I don't think he'll do that, quite
honestly, Tilly.'

'Why not?'

'Bad for business. That's one reason.'

'Yes, I suppose.' Tilly took herself, tall and lonely, away to
another part of the house to spread her story.

No-one was particularly interested. The term was ending
within the next three days and everyone was packing their

soiled clothes into bags and suitcases, since Claire the house-maid refused to have her washing machine choked up with piles of last-minute laundry bundles. Chris had written to his mother: 'I'm getting so used to this desk here in my room, do you mind if I stay here at least part of the holidays? There's plenty of recreation – I can get tennis at the hotel along the road and get on with my novel. I have a thousand ideas for it.' His uncle's next letter as well as his mother's confirmed their desire to do anything, make any sacrifice of his compa-ny, to help him with his 'project'. (They both used the same word.) The uncle had written to Rowland who was perfectly happy to keep Chris on at a special increased rate. He and Nina were not going away from home, at least not together, and not very far – so much to be done to the school in the holidays. Chris was all the more convinced that his mother and uncle were having an affair. It didn't bother him; rather, he was relieved to have them off from his family obligations. He was decidedly contented with the news that Célestine Valette was also staying on at College Sunrise. She had been designated 'temporary' as the cook in some vague honour of the fact that she was the sister of the more bureaucrati-cally important Elaine. Célestine was a very practised good Swiss cook. In general the two sisters were much treasured by Rowland and Nina. Célestine was twenty-four years of age. Chris sometimes slept with her. He was the oldest pupil, soon to be eighteen, and felt a certain *droit de seigneur* in this matter.

Before dinner he went along to the room Pallas shared with Mary Foot. Both girls were there, and let him in. 'Give me my book, Pallas.'

She fished out a hard-covered flat suitcase from under the bed, opened it with her code and pulled out a filing-box and four notebooks. Mary had his personal computer on the floor of her hanging cupboard, covered by a shawl, but Chris had no use for it just then. Mainly, he preferred to write by hand since he could do this sitting on a garden seat or on a seat in a park, or lying flat on his stomach under a tree. Chris had many favourite writing positions and places.

Tonight, he intended, after dinner to elaborate on a fictional meeting between the rising assistant diplomat David Rizzio and the elder Savoyard, generous and wise, Bonivard. The more he thought about it the more possible it became that the two should have met and that after David Rizzio's death it would be natural for David's brother Jacopo, seething with vengeance, to approach Bonivard for support. It was a question of building up the character and filling the plausible historical moment. The more Chris thought of these questions the less he thought of Rowland. He dabbled his hands in water, brushed his hair and went in to dinner still thinking of Bonivard.

Rowland said in French, which was their mealtime language, 'What did you all think of the Château de Chillon?'

'Terrific,' said Leg (Pansy Leghorn). 'I'd like to own a castle on a lake. But the dungeon was grim.'

'You could marry a Scottish laird if you want a castle on a lake,' said Opal Gross. Since her parents' finances had failed she dwelt often in her mind on her future: should she make a prosperous marriage? It was not her only hope: she could get a welfare job, train as a nurse.

They ate *pâté*, fish, salad and a creamy home-made cake. Célestine believed in the food she cooked, and the Mahlers encouraged her to feed the school well. Rowland felt it practical not to be mean, and in fact he was naturally large in his domestic habits. He didn't bother his young people about their leaving lights on or eating second or third helpings. Célestine was encouraged to listen to their preferences however bizarre. 'This is Liberty Hall,' said Rowland very often, and Célestine, though herself frugal-minded, did her best to make items such as fish-finger sandwiches look and taste like something *haute-cuisine*.

They chatted about the Prisoner of Chillon all through the meal. Chris cited the dates when he as a Savoyard could well have met young Rizzio at the diplomatic court of the Piedmontese ambassador to which David Rizzio was attached. Rowland guessed that Chris was on to something in the formation and development of his novel. Rowland did not finish his dinner. He was put out, worried. Nina noticed and heard everything with the mounting alarm of one whose suspicions so far have seemed derisory but now appear to be materializing – yes, to be possible, quite probable, altogether real. Rizzio, thought Chris, born 1537, died 1566. Bonivard born 1493, died –? He felt in his pocket for the brochure he had obtained about the Prisoner of Chillon. On it he saw that Bonivard died in 1570. When Rizzio was, say twenty-five, Bonivard was sixty-nine, a truly old man for those days.

As Chris ate his fish and made his mental calculations, Rowland watched him closely. Lisa Orlando said, 'Chris has gone off into a dream.'

'No,' said Chris, 'I was thinking of something. Literally not a dream, Lisa.'

'What was the boat trip like?'

'Smooth,' said Chris.

'A stunning First Mate,' said Leg.

'No, that was the Captain,' said Pallas.

In 1566, thought Chris, Jacopo Rizzio was eighteen, nineteen. Bonivard was seventy-three. He would have been moved by the young man's story of how his elder brother, the gifted young musician and diplomat, had been brutally murdered with multiple stab-wounds by a savage gang of Scots.

'Make conversation, Chris,' said Rowland.

'There was a party on the boat from the Beau Rivage,' Chris said. 'A group from a psychiatrist's convention. Mixed nationalities. Men and women. Rather wrapped up in themselves.'

'They are not psychiatrists,' said Lionel Haas, 'they are psychologists. I managed to talk to one or two.' Lionel was almost the brightest pupil in the school. He came near to Lisa Orlando, who, at her former school, had been an excellent exam-passer. The two got on well together. Lionel was to stay with Lisa at her parents' house on Elba for part of the summer break. The holidays were on the minds of most of the pupils, now. Princess Tilly was going to stay with an uncle in Roumania. Pallas was joining her father, but whether in Athens or elsewhere, it was impossible to discern from her various statements. (It was widely believed at College Sunrise that her father, George Kapelas, was a spy.) Opal Gross, who was rather feeling the benefit of being of a ruined family, in that offers of help came pouring towards her, was going on a luxury cruise of the Aegean, the Dardanelles and the Greek islands in the yacht of a family friend. Pansy Leghorn was going to a three-week literary summer course at Cambridge after which she would join Mary Foot for a short stay at her family home, a long, low, group of bashed-together alms cottages in Worcestershire. Joan Archer was going to lie on the sundeck round a pool at Juan les Pins with her handsome father, his girlfriend and small brother.

Jacopo Rizzio, thought Chris, would be wearing a thick dark green wool stuff jacket as he has just come from Scotland. Maybe a shawl, not tartan, oh, God. François de Bonivard would have a thick beard, grey and white. I wonder if there's a portrait of him somewhere?

'Rowland – some salad?' Nina said.

Rowland sat on, not eating, unnoticed, while Chris thought out his new chapter and the others chattered of Chillon in the recent past and the holidays in the near future.

VI

CHRIS WAS ENJOYING his solitary position at College Sunrise. With the view of the lake and the French alps, it felt like a luxury hotel. Some mornings after he had worked a few hours on his novel, he wandered along the lake shore to various hotels where he would sit in the bar observing the passing scene, listening to the chatter of English and German package-tourists. He would sip white wine or Coca-Cola. In one hotel he would play chess with an old man on a lawn-chessboard. He took notes. In another, once, he lolled at the bar and read carefully through their brochure; then, with his fine-pointed, clever biro he changed their advertised 'Fitness Room' to 'Fatness …', and did so on the entire pile of brochures under the eye of the barman, who saw but simply didn't notice. Chris was always impressed by the non-noticing faculties of people.

When he left his room at College Sunrise to go out, Chris blatantly locked the door.

'We can't get in to clean,' Nina complained.

'Does it matter?'

'No-one's going to steal anything,' the maid, Claire Denis, said with great indignation.

'Madame Denis, come and make my bed,' Chris said. 'Try to come early before I go out. All I want to protect is my work.'

29

'What should I want with Monsieur's papers?'

'Nothing. Monsieur Rowland might want to see them.'

She said nothing until she had made the bed. Then 'Monsieur Rowland does not write. He sits and looks at the words on the computer.'

Chris was impressed by her noticing faculty, so unlike the barman at the hotel.

'I daresay,' he said, 'that Monsieur Rowland is thinking. When one writes a book one has to think. Or perhaps he's thinking of the school. It's an enormous responsibility.' Chris stressed the word *énorme* in a way that provoked Claire Denis to look at him sideways. 'No kidding,' said Chris. This was the end of the conversation. Nina looked round the door. 'Oh there you are,' she said to Claire. The students were discouraged from 'fraternizing' with the domestic helpers. It could lead to difficulties.

Nina sat in the office with her lists of lecturers. It was early morning, before anyone was up. The school itself was now fairly empty. All the pupils except Chris had left. Albert, the odd-job gardener was on holiday. The sisters Elaine and Célestine Valette were still at College Sunrise. Claire Denis did not live in the college.

Nina had her lists of scholars before her. She had the job of arranging next term's lectures. These generally included overnight visits from a few professors or university lecturers. Nina felt they were the most attractive part of the school's curriculum. She regarded scholars with awe, as if they were so many orders of angels, thrones, Dominations, Powers, Cherubim, Seraphim: Dr D. Dabbler of Southampton University, lecturer in French Provincial Art, Dr Savoie Laroche of Reading, lecturer on the English Potteries, Dr Laura Markoff of Cambridge, lecturer in the Bayeux Tapestries. The subjects were innumerable, the sacred lecturers were equally numerous but not equally affordable. To Nina it was of course impossible that scholars could have ideas of their value above their actual worth, which was anyway priceless. It was only that some were happy to come more or less for the trip away from home, with a moderate fee thrown in, and others wanted a fat pay-cheque.

Then, on another set of lists came the politicians. Nina let her mind soar above the clouds to the realms of the Archangels, Tony Blair, God, but finally she returned to the realistic earth with a choice of three old pensioners, one an undersecretary of something from two governments back, a woman liberal party activist and a brilliant ex-politician brought low by brothel-haunting revealed. Nina felt the latter would have to be passed over in the interests of the school's morals, fascinating though he might be.

Apart from her print-out lists of possible lecturers, Nina had some sets of old card indices on file from some years back when she and Rowland had first started their school. She rummaged in a drawer of her desk and found the cards, bound together by an elastic band. They were the names of older writers, lecturers, retired politicians. Nina meant to have a look through them to see if there was some name she could add to her present autumn-term list. But it seemed to her that the bundle of cards was thicker than she had remembered it to be. She flicked through them. Yes, there were the old names: Dr Alice Barclay-Good. An interesting scholar of sixteenth century Scottish History, she had given a monologue-type lecture to the school when it had first started in Brussels. She was dull. She was, however, docile about money and didn't mind travelling tourist class. All these and many other factors had to be taken into account when inviting a scholar to lecture to the school. However, Dr Alice

Barclay-Good was now retired, like many others on the card index. Probably too much on the old side.

Nina flicked to another card, Alistair French, expert in city-planning. Not much good for the present group of students, but she would keep him in mind. Next, Robert K. Wellington, Jr., Bath Equipment Illinois, telephone ... e-mail ... '*Who?*' said Nina aloud. Who is he? She noticed that the card was slightly creamier in colour than the regular ones. There were other creamy cards, too, in the batch she was holding in her hands. She pulled these out: there were twenty-four of them. 'M. B. Squire, M.D., B.Sc., Birmingham. Aspirin and Klear-a-kold 300 mg.', 'Mrs Thomas A. Watchworth, Belfast, Irish linen,' 'Lord Barbouries' Dairy Farms. Pork pies. Salted butter.', 'Angelique Denis, embroidered towels ...' A card index of merchants and merchandise. How did they get among Nina's scholars and lecturers?

The riddle as to how these cards got among Nina's pack upset Rowland and put him off his novel-writing. 'Who could have been tampering with our office material?'

'I can't think,' Nina said.

'Could it be Chris?'

'Chris? Why should it be Chris?'

'He asked me how my novel was getting on.'

'All right, he asked you how your novel was getting on.'

'You're right. It wouldn't be Chris. I wonder if he's going to feel lonely this summer all alone working on his novel.'

'It's what he wants, Rowland.'

'We could take him to a nightspot in Geneva. I hear there's a Japanese trio, two guitars and a singer. He'd enjoy that, with oriental food to go with it.'

'Great,' said Nina.

Rowland put on his reading glasses and looked closely at the alien creamy cards, one by one. 'Somebody's joke?' he said.

'If so, I don't appreciate it.' He sat down studiously by the phone and quizzed International Directory Enquiries about the names, one by one. 'Thomas A. Watchworth, Belfast, Irish Linen dealer.' Rowland spelt it out letter by letter and waited, and waited. Finally: 'No Thomas A. Watchworth in Belfast? – Don't go away. Try Lord Barbouries' Dairy Farms, somewhere in Cornwall, England. No, I haven't got the name of a town, it's a farm.'

No luck with any of them. The apparent merchants and business people on the cards evidently didn't exist. Rowland said, 'It's a hoax. Just keep them by you.' As he turned them over to Nina he caught sight of the back of the last card. It had the number 5. Another card was 82. There was no particular sequence.

'I didn't notice the numbers,' Nina said.

'Nor me. It's someone playing a game. Ignore it,' Rowland said.

He didn't ignore it. He brooded on it, convinced that Chris had put the cards there for some reason ... No, not for some reason, he had done it *for no reason at all*. And that was the thing about Chris that left Rowland sort of mentally out of breath and completely thrown. He admired, envied, resented Chris with his easy talent and throw-away habits of amusing himself. But was he amusing himself? Whose cards had he mixed with Nina's? But, he thought, not a word will I say. Only I'm on the watch. On the watch, but what for?

Rowland typed:

The girl with the violin. She comes to the local private school to give violin lessons. She sees, standing by the window, a tall, dark boy, who glances up. He is Robert (? George ? Trevor). Anyway, he is the Boy who passes the Window.

At her end of the office Nina quietly tidied away her work. She got up to go, not meaning to disturb Rowland. However, he said, 'I wonder if Chris –'

'You have to get him off your mind,' she said.

Nina was tall, her dark hair hung straight to her shoulders. She had deep, dark greyish eyes with well-balanced facial features. There was something studious about her appearance that made her slightly too intelligent-looking to be a beauty.

She had graduated with honours and most of her imaginative life circled on that fact. She had married Rowland largely because of her esteem for scholarship. His thesis on the German poet, Rilke, had clinched the deal so far as her consent to marry him was concerned. The fact of his academic achievements stimulated her sex life. He, on the other hand, was in love, basically, with her practical dependability. It had been her idea to run a finishing school. She had wanted him to call himself Dr Mahler, but he had sensed that the title would interfere with his main ambition: to write a wonderful novel.

Rowland, too, was tall; he was well-built, with a crop of hair neither dark nor fair and a blade-like face which he occasionally framed with a pointed beard. At the present time he had shaved his face clean, feeling more like a brilliant young novelist under this appearance.

The strain of Rowland's efforts to cope with his novel was felt more by Nina than by Rowland himself. He confidently talked of 'authors' birth-pangs', 'writers' block', 'professional distractions' (reading the school essays); he was full of such phrases, so much that Nina in her accesses of sympathy would even invent them for him. 'How can you give a creative writing course,' she said, 'while trying to write creatively yourself? No wonder you feel put off, Rowland.'

'Yes, it's almost impossible,' he said, 'to describe a process you are actually involved in.'

Nina said, 'I could teach the creative writing class if you like.'

'No. Chris would feel let down. I want to keep my eye on Chris. Besides, for the fees we're asking they expect a creative writer, and, I'm afraid, a man.'

Nina was aware that what he said was more or less true. As an act of will, she gave Rowland her full sympathy, but she knew it contained a built-in time limit. There is a way out, she would tell herself at times. At the end of some school year I could comfortably leave him. In the meantime let him write his novel; it might even be good.

In the meantime: 'Dear Dr Shattard,' wrote Nina. 'You will recall that you gave a distinguished lecture to College Sunrise in Brussels, entitled "Henry James and the European Scene". I am writing to ask if you would come to College Sunrise where it is now situated at Ouchy, Lausanne, and give the same or a similar lecture to a new group of our students. Our term begins ...' She looked up and saw Rowland, at the other end of the room, playing with his novel on the computer. She decided to leave him alone with his creative thoughts.

VII

ONE SUNNY AFTERNOON during the holidays a man in smart white casual clothes, accompanied by a young girl who hopped along with the aid of a stick, came up the path of College Sunrise. He was about thirty, she in her late teens.

Elaine Valette opened the door. The couple introduced themselves: Giovanna and Israel Brown. It was exactly six-thirty in the afternoon.

'Mr Mahler came to see us,' said Israel, 'and so we have come to see him.'

They were soon settled with Nina and Rowland on the terrace sipping drinks in the lovely evening air with the sun slanting over the western mountains.

'Giovanna gave one of your students a fright with her ghostly violin,' said Israel. 'In fact, she was bored. She hurt her leg and had to sit with it up.'

'My young friend gathered so,' said Rowland. 'That was his guess.'

Giovanna was drinking a citron pressé, the others vodka-tonics which Rowland had brought out to them.

'It's good to see neighbours,' Nina said. 'We see few people who live here. Of course, the hotels are full of come-and-go people.'

'You are listed as a finishing school. What exactly is a finishing school?' said Israel.

'Generally,' said Rowland, 'it's a place where parents dump their teen-age children after their schooldays and before their universities or their marriages or careers.'

Giovanna said, 'Polished off?'

'Something like that,' Nina said. 'We try to instruct them, though. I get scholars to come and lecture.'

'Who is the red-haired young man who was serenaded by Giovanna?'

'I wouldn't say red,' said Nina. 'I'd say his hair was orange. He's very brilliant. He's writing an historical novel.'

'Is it good?' said Israel.

'So far as we know,' Rowland said. 'Lately he's being very secretive about it. I think he's probably lost his way.'

'Not him,' said Nina. 'Not Chris.'

'Floundering around, that's what,' said Rowland. 'What can you expect at seventeen?'

Chris thought, when he heard of this visit at dinner-time, They might have asked me to join them. Pigs. So he said, 'Today I managed to complete two long chapters. Difficult ones.'

Rowland smiled, but put down his knife and fork definitively. 'When are we going to see them, the new chapters?'

'Oh, now I'll wait till the book's finished.'

He thinks it is a game he is playing with Rowland, Nina reflected. He doesn't realize how seriously Rowland is affected. She looked at Rowland's unfinished supper and felt a wave of panic. She was afraid that something was happening to Rowland beyond explanation, with which she would be unable to cope.

'Chris,' she said, 'you know, that violinist is a pretty girl. You'd like her.'

'A bit too old for him,' said Rowland. 'She must be eighteen, nineteen …'

'I might go round and see,' said Chris cheerfully.

'Good idea,' said Nina. 'Take a rest from your book.'

'Oh yes,' he said, for all the world as if he was an established man of letters. He spoke English now. 'One does have to pause from time to time, if only to take stock of what one has written and where one stands.'

That repetitive use of 'one' nettled Nina. 'I suppose one does,' she said.

Chris went for a walk after dinner, dutifully reporting the fact to Rowland.

At the house of the violin everything was dark.

None the less Chris went up to the door and pressed the bell. After a while there appeared from round the side of the house the same elderly caretaker.

'You are looking for M'selle and Monsieur Brown?'

'That's right. I'd like to see them.'

'They left an hour ago, or an hour and a half ...'

'Oh, will they be back?'

'One never knows. I have no information. They received your last message.'

'Yes, I know.'

'Do you find,' said Rowland to Chris, 'that at a certain point your characters are taking over and living a life of their own?'

'I don't know what you mean,' Chris said.

'I mean, once you have created the characters, don't you sort of dream of them or really dream of them so that they come to you and say "Hey, I didn't say that."'

'No,' said Chris.

'Your characters don't live their own lives?'

'No, they live the lives I give them.'

'They don't take over? With me, the characters take over.'

'I'm in full control,' Chris said. 'I never thought they could have another life but what I provide on the typed page.

Perhaps the readers, later on, will absorb them in an extended imagination, but I don't. Nobody in my book so far could cross the road unless I make them do it.'

'How strange. Most creative writers and novelists feel quite the opposite. That's the usual experience. That's how I feel too, with my characters, I feel bound to say.'

'Well, I'm a beginner,' Chris said.

Rowland could have stabbed the boy for his modesty and calm. He walked away. He left Chris alone for two days, speaking to him only briefly at meal times. But Rowland was off his food, he wasn't well.

'Every writer gets writer's block,' Nina said. 'That should be an essential theme of one of your creative writing talks. There must be a known way to deal with the situation.'

'I haven't got writer's block,' Rowland said. 'It's only that my characters are so real, so very real. They have souls. If you are writing a novel from the heart you have to deal with hearts and souls. The people you create are people. You can't control people just like that. Chris is writing a novel where he controls people.'

'Oh leave Chris out of it. What do you know about him, after all? In five years' time he might be working in a private bank, managing a sandwich company, teaching history, anything.'

'He told me he controls his characters. He creates them and they have no lives of their own.'

'Well,' said Nina, 'they haven't of course.'

'He doesn't see them as flesh and blood, as human.'

'Well,' said Nina more emphatically, '... flesh and blood – the author can always kill off a character. It isn't a crime. Chris is writing about historical figures, anyway. They killed each other, those characters. What are you worried about?'

'His way of going on with his book makes my No. 3 creative writing lecture look silly.'

'You could change it.'

'Perhaps I'll modify it. How does he mean, he has control of his characters? He didn't create Mary Queen of Scots and her little musician. They're taken out of history, aren't they? They're ready-made.'

'I don't think so, Rowland,' said Nina. 'From the bit we've read, his Mary Queen of Scots, his Darnley and Rizzio, are his. He's already said to me that he doesn't care a damn if Bonivard was probably an invalid after spending six years in the Castle of Chillon. Chris said, "He's as healthy as I make him." The only thing he wants to be precise about is the state of the weather on the day that Rizzio's brother came to Geneva to see Bonivard, and the weather when Darnley was murdered, and always, always, the weather. He says it gives an authentic background.'

'Quite right, I advised that myself, in my second lecture. The weather –'

'So you did. Yes, he must have been listening after all. I always think Chris looks vague when one is teaching.'

'An awfully nice boy,' Rowland said. In his tone was a touch of regret, as if Chris had been an awfully nice dog that however, for some overwhelming reason, had to be taken to the vet to be put down.

VIII

AT COLLEGE SUNRISE, unlike at other, larger, schools of the time in Switzerland, the end of the school year was in mid-December instead of in the summer. Rowland and Nina always arranged a large dinner party and dance for the students, friends and parents, (at their willing expense) with school prize-givings part of the show. This year it was to be held at the nearby five-star hotel. Nina, knowing that the coming term would be full of normal work, was using the school holidays to make preliminary arrangements for the year's final feast.

It was while discussing details of the package with the amiable manager that a thought suddenly struck her which she put at the back of her head to make way for the business on hand. However, on the way home she came back to her thought: I'm running the school alone. Rowland might as well be one of the students. He is hardly one of the staff. He does nothing but his creative writing class now, and hardly that. Originally Rowland had taken Social History, Modern Art and Photography. It was all text-book stuff. Nina found it quite simple to take on these classes when Rowland became immersed more and more in his novel. Simple, but not easy. She had far too much to do. The school fees were very high and the students were entitled to something like what their parents paid for.

At home, Rowland was in the study frowning over his novel. Nina had made up her mind to tell Rowland right away that she was doing much more than her fair share of the school, that she felt overburdened. She sat down at her desk, ready to speak, and she did; but her words that came out were:

'You fancy Mary Foot, don't you?'

'Oh, don't start all that again. Mary's shy. I had to try and bring her out.'

'Well, I think she prefers me to you, if you want an honest opinion.'

'At this moment,' he said, 'I am not taking opinions. I am writing a book.'

'Or is it Pansy?' she said. 'Maybe it's Pansy who keeps you awake.'

Their row blew over, all about something quite different, as it was, from the main cause.

In any case, it was always their quiet, working boarder, Chris, who occupied Rowland's mind. Everything else was peripheral. Rowland told himself that the novel Chris was rapidly producing would be, at best, a popular, not an artistic, success. The fact that Chris was only seventeen – perhaps, when and if the book should be published, eighteen, would stand in his favour. At eighteen a successful historical novelist …

Rowland wrote:

'The two visitors, young aunt and somewhat older nephew, walked sedately up the path.' He took out 'sedately' and put in 'carelessly'. Then he took that out and put in 'casually'. Then he wrote, 'She still had a slight limp.'

But she had been looking for Chris, anyhow. Red-haired Chris.

Rowland, before he had graduated from Oxford, had already written a play for the National Theatre which was a young-person success. It was followed by the offer of play after play by Rowland which, according to his agents, 'you couldn't give away'. He changed agents. They still 'couldn't give away' Rowland's stuff.

His marriage to Nina, and the help of a good legacy, put his nerves to rights for the time being. Their itinerant finishing schools had been satisfying. And now, this lust of Rowland's to write a novel. He was sure he could do it. He remembered the days, eight years ago, when he had achieved the play, and its reception, a month of performances and good critics talking about his future. I am not yet thirty, he reflected. I can make it happen again. A novel has a beginning, a middle and an end. So said Aristotle and so he had advised his creative writing class. A beginning, a middle and an end. Chris had said, 'Do you need to begin at the beginning and end at the end? Can't a writer begin in the middle?'

'That has been tried quite often,' Rowland replied, 'but it tends towards confusion.'

Chris didn't seem to care about this aspect. He seemed to have a built-in sense of narrative architecture and balance.

'Too much individualism,' thought Rowland. 'He is impeding me. I wish he could peacefully die in his sleep.'

I am awfully young, thought Nina, to be tied to a man who is married to a novel. Or perhaps engaged to a novel as it isn't yet real. She longed for Rowland to become Master of an Oxford or Cambridge college. She wanted to be married to a scholar. She had thought he was a playwright when she had married him; that didn't last. But she knew he could never settle to any sort of scholarship. In fact, he was a very good teacher. He got good results, of which Chris was an example. Rowland's novel, she thought, was threatening to break up the school. I am too young at twenty-six to be a wife-psychiatrist, she thought. Let him think of, let him analyse, me. I should have married a scholar. (Eventually Nina, herself, was to become an art-historian, but that was after great effort, and after time ahead ...) Meanwhile at College Sunrise, she was saying to herself, I am married to a state of mind. She decided to tell Rowland she was bored with his novel, but the words that came out were, 'I think Chris went looking for Israel and Giovanna. I wonder if he saw them?'

Chris pondered on the nature of jealousy. He was thinking of Darnley's fierce and primitive jealousy of Rizzio, his wife's favourite, her musician, her confidential friend. In his life he had not yet experienced jealousy at work, although he knew the sensation, and could recognize it in others. He had sometimes envied other boys, and recognized the feeling as a sort of admiration. He knew what it was to want what others had and that he had not, such as a stable family life. And Chris also understood that when it came to looking closely at the thing or condition desired (such as other children's 'stable family life') in fact it didn't seem so very desirable, if indeed it existed at all.

What is jealousy? Jealousy is to say, what you have got is mine, it is mine, it is mine? Not quite. It is to say, I hate you because you have got what I have not got and desire. I want to be me, myself, but in your position, with your opportunities, your fascination, your looks, your abilities, your spiritual good.

Chris, like any of us, would have been astonished if he had known that Rowland, through jealousy, had thought with some tormented satisfaction of Chris dying in his sleep.

College Sunrise was decently but sparsely furnished, with a predominance of good modern Swedish pine-wood. Throughout the house there was a minimum of curtains and cushions. The students stuck posters on their bedroom walls according to their tastes and the bookshelves contained many objects besides books, their private property, including bottles of bath lotion, piles of CDs, wooden carvings, shells, ceramic mugs. The beds were covered with coloured quilts. In the public rooms, as in the bedrooms, there were no carpets. The floors were made of large dark paving tiles, kept in a fairly shiny condition.

The mobile quality of the school was facilitated by this austerity. Visitors from outside found it unaccountably desirable: 'Oh, if only one could always live like this, so calm, so uncluttered, so clean.' It was moveable and cleanable. Nina and Rowland had planned it precisely for this purpose. But Nina sometimes longed for a less functional environment, for rugs and vases of flower-arrangements. She had one comfortable armchair to herself, in the study she shared with Rowland.

She curled up in it while reading aloud a letter that had made her very cheerful. It was from Pansy Leghorn's mother. The girl had left the Cambridge summer course after four days, finding it far too 'bourgeois' after College Sunrise.

'I can't tell you,' she read aloud to Rowland, 'the difference in Leg after her two terms with you. She used to be so stiff and goody-goody, all Girl Guide and Sunday School. I thought she would end up as a clerk in the post office or a woman priest. She actually wore golf-socks over her stockings and oh my God those white blouses. But now I assure you Ms Mahler, you have done wonders for Leg. She has painted the kitchen ceiling green. (The paint got into our lunch, our daily was livid) and she wears skin-tight jeans and skirts up to here. You must know she looks lovely now ...' Nina stopped reading. 'Are you listening, Ro?' Rowland smiled at her. 'Don't I get any of the credit?'

'In fact you do. Listen: "Mr Mahler's course in writing has really got Leg thinking. She took a bunch of newspaper clippings, jumbled them up, took the fifth word out of every printed line and made a fantastic poem. That's freedom of expression Mum she said. And she said you'll never guess how it makes you feel free just to put those words together like that. There's a great meaning when you leave out the grammatical factor. She says Rowland says it's not what you put in it's what you leave out, and it's the silences rather than the sound. I am so grateful for what you have done for Leg Mr Mahler. She's a totally different person. She cut short that summer course at Cambridge of her own free will at her own discretion entirely and I admire her for it. They were teaching that pain in the neck (Leg calls it pain in the ass) George Eliot with the video shows from the BBC production. Leg said that after Mr Mahler's Madame Miss World Bovary she simply couldn't sit there taking in the point about the moral dilemma. The other students were non-profitable to be with, all leadership and laptops ..." – Of course,' Nina said, 'Leg's mother lives in dire wealth.'

'People like her enthuse about everything. But it's true we're a great school,' Rowland said.

'It's so true,' said Nina. 'You really don't need to write a novel. Don't you feel you're one of those people who can get by without writing a novel?'

'No.'

IX

IT WAS WELL advanced into September, the last term of the College Sunrise year. All nine students were settled in again. We find, now, Nina, taking one of her casual afternoon *comme il faut* talks as she called them. Five students lolled around Nina in the large sitting-room: Lionel Haas, Princess Tilly, Lisa Orlando, Pallas Kapelas and Joan Archer.

'In case you are thinking of getting a job at the United Nations,' Nina told them, 'I have picked up a bit of information which may be useful, even vital to you. A senior member of the UN Secretariat passed it on to me especially for you young people. First, if you, as a UN employee, are chased by an elephant stand still and wave a white handkerchief. This confuses the elephant's legs. Second, if chased by a large python, run away in a zig-zag movement, as a python can't coordinate its head with its tail. If you have no time to run away, sit down with your back to a tree and spread your legs. The python will hesitate, not knowing which leg to begin with. Get out your knife and cut its head off.'

'Suppose there isn't a tree to lean against?' Lionel said.

'I've thought of that,' said Nina, 'but I haven't come up with an answer.'

Célestine came in with a large tray of tea and fresh-baked biscuits. She was thin as a wire with black tights and top. Her yellow, bright, hairdresser-done hair fell evenly round her shoulders from a strictly black parting. She and her sister, Elaine, had originated in Marseilles. They both had thin shapes and sharp dark button-like eyes, although Elaine had kept her hair dark. Everyone knew that Célestine was Chris's girl, but nobody, including Nina, was quite sure about Elaine, the older sister, who had opportunities to sleep with Rowland. Did she take them?

Nina often wondered about this, but did not bother unduly. With Elaine teaching French and coping with the computer, and Célestine doing the wonderful cooking, Nina left well alone. Without the wirey girls with their spidery legs what would the school have done?

Célestine spread out the cups and saucers and the plates of biscuits which began to disappear even as she did so. One of the girls poured the tea, another handed round the cups. All was right with the world.

*

All was right with the world for Chris. He now ignored all classes, lessons, lectures of any sort. He knew that Nina and Rowland couldn't afford to send him away from the school, and in any case he also knew he had Nina's affection. As to Rowland, he continued to sense an unnatural curiosity bearing in on his actions, particularly his writings. Chris was quite sophisticated enough to question in his thoughts if this invasive interest of Rowland's was sexual. He decided, perhaps it was, basically, in the sense that sex is basic, but that Rowland had no actual sexual motive or intention. Rowland's interest in Chris was developed, mature, complex. In realizing this, Chris was flattered, and thought better of himself than was warranted. For his book, he did not feel it necessary to follow the historians in every small particular. He was quite capable of making history work for him, his plot, his characters. To Chris, those six years of Bonivard's imprisonment at Chillon from 1530 to 1536, had turned him into a socialist of his time. Well, why not? This made him all the more amenable, in his advanced age, to turn a benevolent gaze on the young Jacopo Rizzio who came to remind him of their meetings at the ambassadorial court of Savoie and other places, when David Rizzio was alive. Bonivard was seen to recall David's musical talents, his diplomatic abilities and charm, and was infuriated against the Scottish Lord Darnley ('leader of the powerful Scottish establishment and husband of the Queen'). Bonivard promised Jacopo help: men, munitions, money, horses, and brains adept at intrigue. They would cross to Scotland secretly, silently, arrange a mass of explosives, and blow up Darnley.

And the Queen, Mary Queen of Scots? Chris pondered deeply whether to make her, too, a socialist at heart. In which case she would be a justified part of the plot. Or was she completely innocent of the murder, but still a leader of the Scottish establishment? Chris felt that Bonivard would have sympathized with the Queen, in the light of her ultimate imprisonment by Queen Elizabeth in England. It had lasted far longer than his, and ended tragically. Chris felt he had to make Mary a rebel, on the side of the victimized Rizzio faction, and certainly, even the straight history books bore witness to Mary's distress on the brutal massacre of her serv- ant. How to prove she was a rebel at heart, socially speaking? Chris decided not to explain this factor.

Princess Tilly was writing a thesis on the massacre of the Nepalese royal family in recent years. She had met one of their remote cousins at the Plaza Hotel in New York. This gave her confidence to describe the already well-documented scene, as if she herself had been there. She had forgotten the name of the young man she had met and dined with at the Plaza, but she made out it was a secret not to be revealed. She called him 'R'. 'As I danced in R's arms, little did I dream of the drama awaiting him back at the Royal Palace ...' In fact there had been no dancing at the Plaza, and the youth in question was nowhere near Nepal when the King and Queen were slaughtered by the distraught Crown Prince, but Tilly was already launching herself excellently on her future journalistic career. Rowland marvelled as he read her essay. How slick and self-confident these young people were ... How they could cover the pages, juggling the paragraphs around on their PCs and never for a moment thinking that any word could be spelt other than the way they wanted it to be. Tilly 'dansed' with her friend from 'Nipall'. Why not? Rowland thought. She will always have an editor to put her story straight. And if only, thought Rowland, I could know what Chris is composing, there alone in his room from which he emerges with that sly and cheerful smile: 'No, Rowland, you can't see it. To show it to you at this stage would ruin it for me.'

Rowland regretted his early efforts to persuade Chris not to write the book. That had been a mistake. At least Chris would have felt at ease to show him what had been written so far, and he would know. Because, of course, Chris did have a plot, he had a construction in mind. People would read that book if it ever came to light, imbecilic as it might be as a historical novel. Chris might, might certainly, might almost surely, succeed in some way. Rowland had an urge to tip a bucket of green paint over Chris's red hair. Green paint, and it all running over his face, and obliterating his book. Or perhaps to wreck the computer with the whole work in it. Switch it off, wreck, terminate it.

Nina now perceived that Rowland's jealousy was an obsession. She believed firmly that Rowland could write a good novel if he was free of jealousy, envy, rivalry, or whatever it was that had got into his mind when he had first encountered young Chris. It was a real sickness, and Rowland would be paralysed as a writer and perhaps as a teacher unless he could get over it.

'Put it away until after Christmas,' she advised Rowland.

'Why?'

'Chris will have left us. He'll have gone home to his mother and uncle, those love-birds, with his novel and his p.c. and his wild ambitions and his red hair.'

'I thought you liked him.'

'Oh, I do,' she said. 'I sort of love Chris.'

'Why do you want him out of the way?'

'He's in your way. His novel-writing bothers yours.'

'Not at all. You haven't understood a thing. It's as his literature and creative writing teacher that I'm anxious about Chris. He's going to be terribly disillusioned.'

'I understand that's a beginner's fate in the world of letters. You should read some literary biographies.'

'You don't believe in me then?'

'Oh, I do. You've got sensitivity and imagination. Also, of course, the know-how. Do you remember that girl Rosie Farnham we had at school in Brussels? How good she was in the creative writing class, remember? – Well, I saw an article of hers the other day in the *Tatler*. Very professional and good, really good. That's thanks to your teaching.'

'What was the article about?'

'How to make a goldfish pond.'

'I remember Rosie. The courier-express family.'

'Yes, well she's a journalist now.'

He sat down at his desk, and she went out, hoping he would break through his writing block.

He remembered now, that Nina had recently suggested: 'Why don't you write about Chris and get him off your chest?

... Just make notes about him – anything that comes into your mind. No-one will know about it. Put down anything you observe.'

It was the creative writing course swerving back on him. Yes, it was exactly his own advice to students stuck for what to write about. 'Watch for details' Rowland had often said. 'Observe. Think about your observations. Think hard. They do not need to be literally true. Literal truth is arid. Analyse your subject. Get at the Freudian reality, the inner kernel. Everything means something other than it seems. The cat means the mother.'

> Observations: Chris and the house of Israel Brown. The girl and the violin. Was Chris inside the gates, lurking? Could he be a Peeping Tom under the guise of a researcher for his own novel? What was he really up to, sitting around the bar of the hotel next door? He says he's 17 but to me he seems older. Is he 17? Perhaps 19. Pallas Kapelas is not yet 17. Chris is very friendly with her. Does he sleep with Pallas? If so, he's a paedophile – am I right? His novel so called is only a cover. He's into porn day and night.

Rowland was scribbling all this with his biro. Yes, it did make him feel better. Nina was right. He had to get it off his chest.

Later, he said to Nina, 'I'm going to send Chris an e-mail.'

'What for? What about?'

'To warn him I'm on his track. I have to warn him.'

'Oh my God,' said Nina, 'you're going mad.'

'Do I sound mad?'

'Absolutely.'

'Then I won't send him any e-mail message. That's just what he's waiting for. He's waiting to accuse me, that I've gone mad.'

'He doesn't think of you, Rowland.'

'Then why did he put Kapelas's missing cards among our card index?'

'Oh, he does that sort of thing all the time. You know, it's only a guess that it was Chris. It could have been anyone.'

'But it's just like Chris.'

'Oh yes. That's why I say it's quite harmless. Look, Rowland, you know, we can't afford to expel Chris from the school. We need every last fee to break even by Christmas.'

'Do we? Why is that?'

'Switzerland is expensive.'

'Well, the fees are too low.'

'No, they're the highest we can get,' Nina said. 'But don't worry. We'll break even with perhaps a profit, after all.'

'You were just trying to frighten me?'

'Well, yes, perhaps a bit. When you go on about Chris … It's all so unreal. And yet, when you see him around, and at meals, you treat him quite normally, so he hasn't the slightest idea that you have an obsession about him. It is an obsession.'

'It is and it isn't,' Rowland said. 'I'm keen to do my writing, finish my novel.'

Nina said nothing. He had hardly started the novel, and was apt to make a new start every now and again. Nina had a much longer-term prospect in mind, which she kept to herself, for she was convinced that sooner or later she would separate from Rowland, marry again, have children, study. But in the meantime, shrewd woman that she was, she knew there was a life to be lived as comfortably and pleasantly as possible. It was mainly, at this moment, a question of trying to keep Rowland's state of mind from running away with itself. Chris, only Chris? Was Rowland an unconscious homosexual? It would be strange if this were so, considering the very perceptive views of life that he held in all other respects.

To be sexually jealous over a man or a woman was something Nina understood, but jealousy over a book, a work of art, a piece of writing ... That was indeed a fact she was trying to swallow. Rowland was simply going mad with jealousy about the writing of novels. It was a fact, not merely a possibility, not something new in the world, but something new to Nina as she grasped it.

X

IT WAS NOT long before Rowland told Nina he had changed his mind about the type of book he was writing. She took a vague note of this. Nina was occupied mainly with guiding her students along the paths that would lead to their future careers. So she told herself but, in fact it was the school that kept her stable. Rowland's secretary Elaine, who was also an excellent French teacher, seemed now to spend less of her time with Rowland and more with very handsome Albert the garden boy. Well, after all, Elaine had always liked gardening. Albert as a close companion was out of bounds to the girl students, for the single reason that Nina was afraid that one of them might get pregnant while in her care.

At dinner that night Opal Gross reported new developments in her family's difficulties: 'My father's really in trouble. Mum thinks he'll go to prison.'

'But he's declared himself a bankrupt, hasn't he?' said Pallas. 'That's a great position to be in.'

'Well, perhaps it's not all as straightforward as that,' said Opal.

'My father can help,' said Pallas.

'What?'

'I know he can help. He buys bankruptcies. He buys and sells them.'

'Pallas,' said Nina, 'it sounds a bit slippery, all that. But of course anything you can do, anything you and your family, or any of us, can do for Opal, we as a school will be very grateful – won't we, you young people?'

Nina had been slightly dismayed by Pallas's cool claim, but her appeal to the dining-table as a whole was being greeted with warm assent, real enthusiasm. She said, 'Get a message to your father, Pallas. Let's see what he can do. I must say I never heard of buying and selling a bankruptcy before – did you, Rowland?'

'No,' said Rowland, 'but I've heard of it now. Why not?'

'Bankruptcies pay a percentage. You buy low and sell high,' said Chris, 'and you don't have to pay your bills any more.'

'I have some cards that probably belong to Pallas's father,' said Nina. 'They got mixed up in my index-box with schol-ars' cards.'

'I think they should be handed back to Mr Kapelas,' Rowland said.

Rowland later wrote in his book of Observations:

Chris knows all about fraudulent bankruptcy. How did he come by this knowledge? Is he the son of a fraudulent bankrupt?

He said to Nina as soon as she put in an appearance, 'I've changed my mind, you know, about the book I'm writing. It won't be a novel. It will eventually be a life-study of a real person, Chris. At present I am accumulating the notes.'

'Well, that's quite a sweet idea,' she said. 'A study of a clever teenager. You'll have to keep it anonymous. Chris wouldn't like it.'

'Oh, yes, anonymous.'

She almost panicked, but set herself strongly to remind him of the forthcoming evening's activities. They had planned a fashion-show with a cat-walk. Everyone in the school was to take part with their best clothes. The cat-walk had been set up in their big common room.

By any standards the fashion-show that evening was a glorious success. The room had been transformed into the image of a veritable fashion-house. In the resulting home-movie it looked quite the real thing. Strategically stacked banks of convincing paper flowers, regardless of their seasonability, were placed in all parts of the room. An unnecessary fire was glowing and flickering luxuriously. Makeshift screens, over which were draped multi-coloured bed-covers, were mostly due to the work of Elaine and Célestine, with the support of the daily maid Claire and Albert the garden boy with his pine-wood branches for uprights.

The cat-walk itself was composed of two long kitchen table tops which were conveniently separable from their legs, as were most of the college tables. These were mounted on wooden boxes and flanked by clusters of plants. Seats were lined up on either side. A bar, offering fruit juices, Coke and sweet petit-fours was set up in one corner with Mozart playing softly in another.

Light-bulbs had been obtained which allowed for many varieties of illumination, from dim to dark to glowing to bright, throughout the room. Lionel Haas and Rowland were responsible for the impressive lighting throughout the show.

The only guests from outside the school were Israel Brown (his young aunt was away) and the manager's wife from the hotel next door (her husband was too busy) who had agreed to be judges of the show. They were joined on one line of side-seats by Nina, Elaine and Célestine, Claire the maid and Albert. At each end, conveniently placed for their intermittent operations on the lighting, were Rowland and Lionel.

The opposite row of seats was sporadically occupied by the models themselves: all nine students. As each took to the cat-walk another sprang up and disappeared behind the screens.

Chris was the Master of Ceremonies. 'Oh, Ladies and Gentlemen,' he announced, 'We are about to present our Sunrise fashion show, confident that our styles will soon become famous throughout Ouchy and beyond.' He wore a dark suit, white shirt and large green floppy bow tie.

Princess Tilly was first on the walk, tall, with her dark hair piled up, mysteriously elegant in a brown and gold antique shawl which she later revealed came from Cambodia. She wore the shawl wrapped round her waist to the effect that it revealed one of her high-stepping legs in their stiletto heels. She was practically topless under a transparent blue scarf, the possible perception of her toplessness to the audience depending on the lighting-scheme. She walked, stopped, dramatically swivelled and walked back with great style, already followed by Mary Foot, less beautiful but equally spectacular. She, too, wore a shawl draped to serve for a dress. She was all in white. Rowland was very careful with Mary's lighting, so that her short white fur boots kicked out clouds of the white chiffon shawl. Mary was a pale, tallish wisp, with long, naturally fair hair falling almost to her waist. She adored Nina and Rowland, especially because he wrote her letters for her at her dictation. Mary was totally unable to spell or write in any language, including her own. She could start a letter Dear Dad, but never got as far as Dad, being unsure whether to put Dere, Dear, Deer or maybe Dier or Dior. It puzzled her so much that she became almost ill if she had to write or type a message. Her experience of the hilarity which her many attempts had hitherto provoked, in schools and out of them, altogether unnerved her. She had been put through many forms of treatment without success. She had very little to guide her where words were concerned. She spoke well and clearly, without trouble, but she simply could not turn speech into spelling, having neither a phonetical ear nor a photographic eye for it. Rowland always took down her messages and conveyed them with great kindness and pleasure. He discerned that she could mentally photograph a few short slogans and was quite good at prices. He therefore predicted for Mary a successful career in the village shop that she craved, selling ceramics and transparent scarves. She would also be an adorable wife and mother, he told her. She loved Rowland for all this. She had never felt so confident, and now that he was manipulating the lighting for her cat-walk appearance, she felt as radiant as she looked.

Rowland's eyes were on Chris, now, announcing, 'Our stunning No. 3, the stately brown-haired model Joan Archer whose …' His voice was lost in the applause as Joan, stately indeed, and decidedly robust compared to the first two girls, stepped forth in a black satin sheath with bare shoulders. She wore a dog-collar of fake diamonds from the local supermarket and a pair of long green gloves. Joan was very swingy. She was hoping to be accepted in a drama school next year. Chris, watching her, thought she might be a good Mary Queen of Scots in the motion picture of his novel.

But then came Lionel Haas himself, relieved from his double duty as lighting assistant, to Rowland. He wore a flowered shirt and shorts, satin, with a dark background, a pair of long, white-rimmed sun glasses, a soft panama hat and gold leather sandals. Picking up his seaside summery statement, Pallas Kapelas followed wearing a minimal grey bikini. She wore rimless sun glasses and she, too, wore gold sandals. Less confident than the girls who had preceded them, both Lionel and Pallas none the less put on an attractive performance, with much elegant elbow and footwork.

Opal Gross, being tiny, had thought well to project her presence with an enormous, high, cone-shaped hat, covered with flowers, feathers, shells, heads of corn and small pine cones. She wore a simple Greek-style tunic that she had brought back from her Aegean holiday, with bare legs and feet. As Chris announced Opal he observed over the top of her hat the faces of Nina and Israel Brown smiling at each other with extreme affability at the same time as they joyfully applauded.

Pansy Leghorn or Leg was also a small girl, but she had decided to be herself in her shell-pink taffeta evening dress, and shoes to match. She wore a pearl tiara and carried a very large box of chocolates under her left arm. As she kicked her skirts out on the cat-walk, there flashed glimpses of a black frilled petticoat.

Chris had slipped away, and now it was near his turn. He had not changed from his dark suit, white shirt and floppy green tie, but he brought with him on his arm Lisa Orlando with her shiny black bobbed hair and golden skin. Lisa was a southern Italian. Chris had arranged to take her with him to make Lionel jealous, as everyone supposed. Lisa wore a green shawl arranged to cover only one shoulder and one breast, reaching to her knees, with glittering glass beads of various colours falling to her feet. She wore green platform sandals, which made her taller than red-haired Chris. They made an emphatic couple. Rowland concealed his fury with Chris from all but Nina, who noticed that the sight of Chris swinging up the fashion gangway with the lovely little Italian girl on his arm had infuriated Rowland. He, in fact, was clutching his throat as if to control a scream.

Albert was on the cat-walk now, in a cream tropical suit with a silk scarf of dark blue and white spots. He had bought it ready-to-wear in the supermarket. It fitted perfectly. In his

breast pocket was the tip of a red silk black-spotted handkerchief and he wore red espadrilles without socks.

'Really – your gardener?' said Israel Brown. Albert looked
fabulously rich. The applause went on so long that he had to
turn round and do it all over again. 'I imagine he won't be
our garden boy for long,' said Nina to Israel. The manageress
of the hotel next door was also carried away by Albert's ele-
gance. She had been appointed one of the judges of the show
and it was in fact eventually to Albert that the first prize was
to be awarded. He was, indeed, a young beauty. And one of
the truths about him was, he was devoted to gardening.

Elaine and Célestine Valette concentrated respectively on
a spectacular raincoat and a tennis dress, the first being a
multi-coloured tent which gave a rainbow effect as Elaine
moved. She wore knee-length red shiny boots and carried
a white closed umbrella. Célestine's tennis outfit resembled
a ballet-dancer's tutu, her two-layered skirt projecting and
bouncing as she moved her tawny stalk-like legs up the walk.

The whole process took place again, more quickly and
boisterously. Finally, Nina and Rowland walked along the
planks, hand in hand, dressed only as they were, bowed to
right and left and retreated to considerable explosive noise
and applause. Refreshments were then ardently served. And
so ended the College Sunrise fashion show.

XI

ACCORDING TO the catechism of the Roman Catholic faith, into which Rowland had been born, six sins against the Holy Spirit are specified. The fourth is 'Envy of Another's Spiritual Good', and that was the sin from which Rowland suffered.

Suffered is the right word, as it often is in cases where the perpetrators are in the clutches of their own distortions. With Rowland, his obsessive jealousy of Chris was his greatest misfortune. And jealousy is an affliction of the spirit which, unlike some sins of the flesh, gives no-one any pleasure. It is a miserable emotion for the jealous one with equally miserable effects on others.

After the fashion show Olive, that manageress of the near-by hotel, who, with Israel, had distributed the prizes had said in her speech, 'How I wish I could have spent part of my youth in a school like yours. And no exams ... It could have been a wonderful memory.'

'And this evening,' Israel added, 'is going to be a wonderful memory.' He smiled at Nina, and she at him. This exchange of smiles was noticed by Rowland. Almost to his own surprise he didn't feel in the least jealous of his wife. He was watchful of Chris who was telling Olive how much he enjoyed sitting in one of the hotel's capacious public rooms, working at peace on notes for his novel.

'You're writing a novel?'

'Oh yes. I'm well ahead with it.'

Olive turned to Rowland, 'You must be terribly proud of your student-novelist. What a distinction for your school –' and turning to Chris – 'Do come any time and use our writing-rooms. You can bring your laptops and things. We'll be delighted.'

'He hasn't got a publisher yet,' said Rowland. 'That's the *sine qua non* of a book.'

'He'll get a publisher,' said Olive, brimming with goodwill and middle-aged glow.

'I could kill him,' thought Rowland. 'But would that be enough?'

Many times, now, Rowland thought of how it would be if Chris were dead. It wouldn't do. It wouldn't be enough. There would always remain the fact that Chris had lived, had been writing a novel while still at school, had prevented Rowland from writing his novel.

Rowland, opening his notebook of Observations on Chris one night before going to bed, found the following words, not his: Watch him at table sitting next to Mary Foot. He is a groper.

Rowland rushed into the bedroom where Nina was already in bed, propped up, reading a book. 'Someone's been meddling with my work,' he said.

'Meddling? How?'

'I've found words in my notebook that I didn't write.'

'I'd say it was Chris,' she said, and went on reading.

'Are you going to let him get away with it?'

'Oh, Rowland, can't you talk to him yourself?'

'No, I'd prefer to put up with him. It's only a couple of months, and he'll be going. Don't let it worry you, then,' he said.

Nothing was worrying her, but she knew he was upset once more by Chris. Only a couple of months to the end of the school year. Nina had spent the afternoon with Israel Brown, not quite in bed, but nearly. She found him attractive, learned, charming, scholarly, sexy.

At dinner the next day, Tilly, with her genius for making unsettling remarks, asked Chris how he was getting on with his novel.

'It's growing,' he said.

'Growing fat,' said Pallas to remind everyone that it was she who kept notes, discs and printed pages of Chris's book as it developed, when he was not working on it.

'Why did Darnley murder Rizzio?' said Mary Foot.

'Jealousy. Rizzio was more interesting to the Queen than her husband was. Rizzio and Darnley were close, confidential friends to start with. But Darnley became obsessed with jealousy.'

'The Queen forgave him for Rizzio's murder?' said Joan Archer.

'She was a politician at that point. She was ...'

He was unusually happy and expressive on his theme, and especially on the question of jealousy. 'Darnley was a tall, handsome fellow. A cousin of the Queen, a royal. It quite appalled him that word was going round, as it did, that Rizzio, small and humbly born, was her lover. Rizzio had a great talent for music, for courtiership. He had already been a diplomat when he'd met Bonivard, or might have met – that's a fictional proposition of course ...'

Rowland was unable to eat, or even of going through the motions of touching food with his fork. He sat immobile. Tilly prodded on:

'It's true you will need a publisher. How do you go about that?'

'Well, as a matter of fact,' said Chris, 'I've got three publishers nibbling already. I'll tell you how I went about it.' And he soon had the table shouting with laughter – (Rowland did not join) – as he told how he had written to the three publishers in London: 'I have just turned seventeen and I am writing an historical novel based on Mary Queen of Scots and the murder of her husband Darnley. The theme is jealousy and passion.' Chris said, 'They all seemed to find this irresistible. I have the feeling that my being seventeen is an attractive part of the deal. One of them has offered to come and see me. Another has offered me a contract on sight of the first ten pages. They're terribly enthusiastic. I can get money for my book.'

'Money?' said Opal.

'Yes, real money. But I won't let that influence me in my choice of publisher.'

'Quite right,' said Mary Foot.

'I don't agree,' said Pallas. 'If they invest money, they will put an effort into publishing the book. The highest bidder should never, never, be entirely ignored. My Pa says so.'

'But a novel is a work of art,' Mary said. 'Or should be. And a work of art is without price. Art comes before commerce.'

Everyone at the table agreed to that. Everyone excluding Rowland, who remained in a catatonic pose, his elbows on the table and his two hands some inches in front of his eyes as if he was amazed at something. He was in fact amazed that those hands would decidedly want to strangle Chris.

'But,' said Nina, 'the labourer is worthy of his hire and so let's hope that Chris will get reasonable pay for his work – Rowland, will you pass down the sauce, please?'

Rowland did not move.

'Rowland ...'

He slowly unwound himself from his trance and pushed the sauce-boat across the table. He said, 'Don't count your chickens before ... well, Chris, they might not accept the book.'

Many protests arose from round the table, but Chris said, 'I might never even live to finish the book, Rowland. How can one know?'

Israel Brown said to Nina, 'He should go on a spiritual retreat. I know of a Catholic monastery in the mountains. They don't try to convert you, they just give peace of mind. If you like I'll get them to arrange something for Rowland. It's obviously what he needs.'

'He's already a Catholic,' Nina said, 'nominally.' In desperation, she had been describing Rowland's condition to Israel on one of her afternoon visits. She had said, 'He needs a psychiatrist,' but Israel had said, 'No, I think it's a spiritual problem.'

'It's difficult, right in the middle of term,' said Nina. 'I'd have to cope alone. But with this obsession ...'

'The boy should leave, of course,' Israel said.

'We can't send him away. We took him on as a sort of apprentice writer. He said he was writing a novel and we agreed. Rowland was supposed to help him. Rowland published an article in his university review and he has had a novel in mind. That's all he's done for three years. He's come to a block. I keep telling him it's nothing to do with his fundamental talent. He genuinely thinks Chris is a menace to the literary profession. A romantic novel from a boy of seventeen will always be popular.'

'Could Rowland be an unconscious gay?'

'He could be, but how would I know?'

'You would know,' said Israel.

'He's hypnotized by Chris.'

'By Chris or by his novel?'

'How would I know?'

'You would know,' said Israel.

'I know you're right,' she said. 'In fact our marriage is all washed up. I'm just waiting till the end of term.'

'Doesn't he know that?'

'Not a bit. He no longer thinks of me, his marriage, the school, or anything at all but Chris, his novel. The students are aware there's something wrong, they're not fools.'

'Can you tell him to his face that he's ill?'

'Not yet.'

It was Chris who told Rowland that he was ill. He had taken it for granted that Rowland knew himself to be in a state of bad nerves. Rowland was sometimes in the habit of taking a long ride on his motor-bike in the mountains in the early afternoons. In the past spring one of the students, very often Chris or Lionel Haas, had accompanied him on the back of the bike. It was good to get the mountain air. Chris had always enjoyed a ride with Rowland. But now when, one afternoon, Rowland said, 'Coming for a spin?' Chris said, 'No, thanks.'

It was a cold, sunny day. Rowland said, 'Come on, Chris, it will do you good. You must get some air.'

'No, thanks, Rowland. Those steep roads are quite dangerous, you know. I honestly don't think you're in good enough shape to take the bike up there. Your nerves ...'

'My nerves? They're all right. What's the matter? Do you think I want to land you over a precipice?'

'No, you wouldn't want to, but you might.'

'You think I would want to kill you?'

'Not really.' They were in the entrance hall, and Chris turned to go upstairs. Tilly was coming down just then.

'Tilly, will you come for a spin in the mountains on the bike?'

'It's our drama class this afternoon,' she said. 'I don't want to miss it.'

It was true that a teacher of drama, a retired actress from Geneva, was due to take her weekly class that afternoon.

'Are you afraid?' Rowland said.

'Afraid?'

'To come on my bike?'

'Of course not, Rowland. But I do like the drama class. It's so marvellous to learn how to arrange flowers that aren't there and talk to someone who actually isn't there, at the same time.' She was dressed in a tight-fitting orange wool dress, very much prepared for her drama class.

Rowland went to Nina. 'I offered Tilly. I offered Chris a ride on my bike, but they won't come.'

'There's the drama class this afternoon,' she said. The drama class was extremely successful. Nina knew that the students wrote home enthusiastically about it. And indeed they were lucky with Mme Sousy de Merier, a born conveyor of the facts and tricks of the profession. Even Chris would leave his novel to participate in Mme Sousy's lessons. 'They can't leave the lessons,' Nina said. 'I won't allow it.'

'But Chris and Tilly are afraid to ride on the back of my bike. I can feel it. I can sense it. Am I in a nervous condition?'

'Yes.'

'How do you know?'

'Everyone knows.'

'Everybody is discussing me?'

'That's not so. And it's neither here nor there.'

'It's Chris. He's getting me down.'

'I'll send him home if you like.'

'Home? Where does he live? I'd only follow him. You don't understand what it's like to feel this compulsion to stop a kid writing an idiotic book. He's got publishers now, on account of his age. Every publisher wants a novel by a red-haired youth of seventeen with a smattering of history and a good opinion of himself.'

'Maybe it's a good novel.'

'Impossible.' Rowland's voice went up to something near a scream.

'Listen, Rowland,' she said. 'I've been talking to Israel Brown.'

'And you're having an affair with him,' he said, suddenly very bored, very weary.

'And you don't care.'

'No, frankly, I don't. Who is he? What does he do?'

'I think he has a gallery. I think he studies art and music. Maybe philosophy ...'

Rowland was not listening. He said, 'I could even take out a boat on the lake and tip all Chris's possessions, all of them including his computer, his discs, his print-outs, into the lake ...'

'And Chris as well,' said Nina.

'Yes, I could tip him over the edge. He stopped me writing my novel. I have a book of observations about Chris that would make you shriek and shiver. I could ...'

'Enough,' said Nina. 'You're ill.'

XII

IT WAS THE end of October and Rowland had been three weeks at the Monastery of St Justin Amadeus on a Swiss mountain plateau near the French border. He was soothed; he was calm. The sound of plainsong three times daily so filled his ear that he found it difficult to rid his mind of the music in between the services. He helped to chop wood every day. He meditated, he prayed.

In these weeks he had written three long essays on the subject of literary composition which Nina, who visited him every other day, had taken back to College Sunrise to be read aloud to the creative writing class in Rowland's absence, by Lionel Haas. Nina brought Mary Foot to visit Rowland several times, and had promised to bring other students to the monastery. These visits, in fact, seemed quite naturally to fit in with part of their education. The white-robed monks moved like automatons about their duties, sometimes separately, sometimes, on their way to the chapel, in single file. The Prior, who had a becoming white beard, caused them to be served carrot juice, which was, he held, a good drink for high altitudes. The friars made a wine which they sold to merchants in the French valleys. On the labels, in English, it was pronounced to have 'a great personality in the mouth, savouring of prunes, tobacco, wild fruits.'

Rowland had managed to put the thought of Chris aside, as something to be dealt with when he should later 'return to reality' as he told himself. When he thought of Chris, he felt a decided simmering of resentment.

But he was now thoroughly bored at the monastery. He knew the Psalms by heart, so that they had become just words, and there was really nobody for him to talk to. The good Prior scarcely appeared outside of the Mass and other services in the chapel. One morning he decided to go home and avoid Chris as much as possible. He was expecting Nina to arrive that afternoon.

He left word with the Prior that he was leaving, wrote a gracious letter thanking the community for their support in his difficulties and made ready to go in to the refectory for his last lunch of barley soup and macaroni-cheese. He crossed the courtyard for this purpose. Around the bend towards the main gate came hooting a Honda piled with a back-seat bundle; it was ridden by a lithe, helmeted youth.

'Hallo, Rowland,' said the youth, and drew up noisily, dramatically, at the doorway.

Rowland peered at his face. The boy took off his helmet and shook his red, red hair.

'Chris.'

'Yes, Rowland.'

'What are you doing here?'

'I phoned the Prior. They've got a place for me.'

'You want to come here?'

'I can't work without you, Rowland. I need whatever it is you radiate. I have to finish my novel in peace.'

'You're mad.'

'And you?'

'I? – I'm going home with Nina this afternoon.'

Chris left his bike in the courtyard and pushed his way through the door into the house. He said, over his shoulder, 'Nina isn't coming this afternoon.'

'Come in and meet the sub-Prior. It's lunch time. Remember this is a religious house.'

The Friar whose duty it was that day to read to the assembled company during their mid-day meal had chosen a passage from the English mystical book *The Scale of Perfection*. Chris listened, absorbed, as he chewed his bread and swallowed his soup, and did not notice when Rowland helped himself to the keys on the table; he didn't notice that Rowland's place was suddenly vacant.

Rowland, in fact, having liberated the Honda from its package by dumping it in the courtyard, was on his way back to Ouchy on Chris's Honda, stopping only to fill up with petrol.

Nina was conducting her *comme il faut* class. 'Be careful who takes you to Ascot,' she said, 'because, unless you have married a rich husband, he is probably a crook. Even if he's your husband, well ... Not many honest men can take four days off their work, dress themselves in a black suit and a silk hat with all the accoutrements, and lose a lot of money on the horses, and take you out afterwards or join a party of people like him. For Ascot you will need warm underwear in case it's cold. You can wear a flimsy dress on top. But your man is bound to be a crook, bound to be. It teems with crooks ...'

'My Dad doesn't go to Ascot,' said Pallas.

'Oh, I didn't say all crooks went to Royal Ascot, only that there are plenty of them at that function.'

In walked Rowland. Célestine, who occasionally became an honorary student, and was to-day participating in this much-favoured lesson of Nina's, let out a cry: 'Monsieur Rowland – but Chris is already on his way to join you at the Monastery of St Justin Amadeus. He needs some literary support.'

'Will someone ring up the monastery and tell Chris I've got his bike here. I borrowed it.'

Célestine said, 'It's time for tea;' she hurried out of the room as if to avoid some explosive situation. But Nina had kept her head.

'Nice to see you back,' she said.

'Don't let me interrupt,' Rowland said. 'I'm just checking in. Do you mind if I join you? – Go ahead.' He sat down amongst them, beaming at Nina.

'I was just winding up,' Nina said. 'I have been describing how one goes about Ascot. And now a word about good manners. If it can be said of you that you've got "exquisite manners", it's deadly. Almost as bad as having a name for being rude. Ostentatious manners, like everything else showy, are terribly bad. If you're a man don't bow and scrape. Never wash your hands in the air as did a late Cardinal of my acquaintance, when trying to please someone. If you're a girl, just show a lot of consideration to the elderly. There's no need to jump to your feet if one of your friend's parents comes into the room, far less your own. It looks too well-trained. Try not to look very well brought-up, it's awful. At the same time, you should consider others round you. Don't be boring as so many people are, who have exquisite manners. Never behave as if people didn't exist. What do you say to that, Rowland?'

'Excellent advice,' he said. 'I'll try to bear it in mind, later in life when no doubt I'll be an S-shaped professor dragging a small suitcase on tiny wheels at an airport.'

Everyone seemed relieved that Rowland's appearance had not caused a crisis. Nina said, 'That's very probable. But I was really about to give advice to any student who is thinking of going into some job where they would have to deal with the public, such as the hotel business, or a shop, or entertainment of some kind. You must learn, first of all – and teach your staff from those in the most humble position upwards – the arts of hypocrisy. In the hotel business it is, to start with, called *accueil*. It involves greeting every newcomer with a welcoming attitude and a modest smile. Let the client believe it means all the world to you that they have arrived in your hotel, your business, your café or whatever.'

'In the same way as you welcome us to the school?' said Tilly.

'A good observation. You're perfectly right. We make you welcome, however frightful your parents are. You yourselves are seldom horrible, as you know. And I must tell you, now, that very often behind the scenes in places of business which have to do with the public, the employers as well as the employees, grumble greatly about the people they have to deal with. These quite understandable, often quite valid, feelings spill over into the business itself. If such an attitude catches on in any place open to the public, and the owners and staff fail to practise the necessary hypocrisy, the business will suffer. People will tell each other "Don't go to that store, the assistants turn their back on you and just go on with their private conversations or they just go on talking to their mums on their phones and ignore you." Same with universities. Nobody wants to listen to a lecturer who is obviously bored with his class. He has to feign enthusiasm.

'In order to succeed with the public you have to be a hypocrite up to a definite point. You will know yourselves when the point has arrived at which you drop all hypocrisy. This can happen. But that's another discourse. On the whole it's best to avoid discussing your clients unfavourably among yourselves.'

'Is it difficult to be a hypocrite?' said Mary Foot. She was thinking of her ceramics shop-to-be.

'Not very much,' said Nina. 'We do it in civilized society the whole time, in fact.'

Opal Gross, her family having faced the financial crash, was in some difficulties about her future. She asked Nina, 'Do you have to be a hypocrite if you have a career in the Church?'

'Oh, yes. What I say applies to the Church very much.'

'The Anglican Church?'

'Any church.' Nina knew that Opal thought of becoming an Anglican priest as a solution to her problems, spiritual and material.

'It's hypocrisy,' said Nina then, 'that makes the world go round.'

Tea was brought in. Nobody noticed that Rowland had left the room.

After dinner that night a taxi drew up at College Sunrise, bearing Chris and his luggage.

'What do I do now?' said Rowland. Chris had gone upstairs with his things. 'What do I do now?' He was in the sitting room having coffee with Nina and most of the students.

'He was bound to come back,' Lionel Haas said. 'He needs a tutor, some creative writing guidance.'

'Did he tell you that?' Rowland said.

'Oh, yes. It's part of his identity as a writer. He started out writing a book with you as his mentor, and it set a pattern. He can't go on without you.'

'What a mad idea,' said Pallas. 'As if Rowland can hover over him all the time. Doesn't he intend to be a writer in the future?'

'Chris isn't really one of our students,' Nina said. 'He's only here to write his novel. I think we should just ignore him. He's free to come and go, so long as we know roughly where he is.'

XIII

DR ALICE BARCLAY-GOOD had agreed to come again and lecture to College Sunrise in the winter term because it made a break in her retirement routine; she would be paid a modest fee and her travelling expenses. She would be put up for the night at the school in Switzerland. She had nothing better to do, and Scottish history of the sixteenth century was very much her subject. She had been invited by the Principal, Nina Parker to speak on the subject of Mary Queen of Scots and her Times. 'One of our students,' went the e-mail, 'is at work on a very original novel on the subject. He already has a publisher and is negotiating the film rights. So we are very proud of him.'

It was true that Chris had been visited by a film producer and a director, both of them staying prominently and luxuriously in the nearby hotel. One was tall and middle-aged, the other short and young. They had spent two days discussing every possibility with Chris, including the casting. But Chris was reticent as to how the book would develop and how it would finish. The producer (the tall one) was anxious about Chris's need for 'much more time'. 'You're seventeen. Under age. That's a selling point. If you wait till you're eighteen, nineteen, you might as well be anybody.'

While these film men were at the hotel they were visited by Pansy ('Call me Leg') who introduced herself as a fellow-student of Chris – 'Maybe I could help you? Call me Leg.'

This ambiguous approach by the small, eager girl earned her a glass of chilled white wine and a promise to bear her in mind for the motion picture script. She impressed on them that she had attended a summer course at Cambridge and that she had the advantage of a rare insight into Chris's working mind.

After the film-makers had left Nina asked Chris what were his intentions now. Did he still want to stay at the college and finish the novel?

'It depends on Rowland.'

'How, "depends on Rowland"?'

'I need him.'

Nina was apprehensive about what he would say next, suspecting that it was something she couldn't handle.

However, Chris went on to say what he had to say next: 'I need his jealousy. His intense jealousy. I can't work without it.'

And Nina, terrified of what she herself would inevitably say next, nevertheless went on to say it. 'Chris, he might kill you.'

'That would be bad for the school,' said Chris.

'Go away,' she said. 'I think I want you to go away.'

'Rowland doesn't.'

How would one handle a situation like this? She and Rowland were joint heads of the school. Nina foresaw the possibilities of a great fuss, a complete break-up of the school with this and that student taking 'sides'. There were weeks ahead till the end of term. Nina had hoped to balance the tension between Rowland and Chris for the remaining period.

'Chris,' she said, 'I believe you are coming to Dr Alice Barclay-Good's lecture?'

'Yes, of course.'

'Will you introduce her?'

'No, let Rowland do that. After the lecture I'll thank her profusely on behalf of the school.' Chris was very much in charge.

Israel Brown had work to do at his London art gallery, but he neglected it on account of his growing attraction to Nina. She seemed to say exactly what he hoped she would say. She handled her plainly psychotic husband with admirable tact and helpfulness, she was a beautiful girl and aware of it. The more he lingered on in his lakeside villa, the more he loved Nina. They made love in the afternoons whenever Nina could free herself from the school, and when she had gone he could feel satisfaction in looking at a wool jacket she had left behind, hanging on a peg in his bathroom, beside his dressing gown. He would have liked to put a frame round the two garments, almost as if they were a picture. In the weeks when Rowland had been at the monastery, Nina had spent whatever hours of her time she could spare from the school with Israel Brown.

The students were hesitantly conscious of this affair although Nina was careful. They were not scandalized if Nina went to swim in Israel's indoor pool rather than the pool in the nearby hotel, where the school often went by special arrangement. It was not Nina's affair that occupied their speculations, but Rowland's obsession with Chris, and Chris's reaction.

Rowland, when he returned from the monastery, resumed a routine of literature and art classes, his creative writing class and his computer-wisdom class and he accompanied them to the gym in the hotel, or to a game of squash. He went for walks along the lake and on steamboat expeditions. Rowland, in fact, helped to fulfil the school's curriculum equally with Nina. But he had become ill-looking, absent.

Mary Foot, who so much adored Rowland, was inconsolable when he forgot her name: 'Opal – Lisa – oh, yes, Mary.'

'I think he's gay and hooked on Chris,' was Lionel Haas's verdict.

'You should be so gay,' said Célestine Valette, the long-legged cook.

Dr Alice Barclay-Good was a tall, built-up woman with a smooth, apple-like face, grey swept-back hair, deep eyes, and was altogether handsome for her age, sixty more or less. Nina had been to the airport to meet her, radiant and proud as she always was when one of her much-admired scholars visited the school. Nina was well-satisfied with the authoritative and confident aspect of her lecturer. She had not changed much.

Rowland had been to their local doctor that afternoon, complaining of a sense of imbalance and stomach unease. He was trembling. The doctor prescribed medicine for Ménière's disease, an affliction of the inner ear which causes dizziness. 'But you suffer from your nerves, don't you?' he added, recalling the number of Rowland's recent visits – more than anyone else in the school put together. He gave Rowland an additional calming drug which in fact rendered him useless for the rest of the day, so that Nina was obliged to introduce the lecturer while Rowland lolled in a front seat, eyes half-closed.

Dr Alice was first introduced one by one to the students. This was to give Nina a chance to explain, when it came to Chris's turn, that he was the star pupil who had already earned the attention of film producers and some newspaper diary paragraphs by writing his historical novel.

'I should have thought Mary Queen of Scots had been exhausted as a subject,' said Dr Alice.

'I have a new theory on Darnley's murder,' said Chris, and he described how it might have been that, with a little help from an imported source, Rizzio's brother, Jacopo, might well have connived at the murder of his brother's killer, Darnley. 'It would be the natural reaction in any Italian family.'

'We must discuss this further,' said Dr Alice, plainly not wishing her lecturing-juice to be used up before the event.

Mary Queen of Scots and her Times was comfortably launched in the cosy, crowded common room. 'The Queen and her Times,' she said 'are closely connected. You know already that Mary was condemned to death on counts of treason and murder. To bring about her downfall, letters and sonnets, known as the "Casket Letters and Sonnets", were produced. It is clear to any legal or even lay mind to-day that these were forgeries. But what you should realize about the intellectuals and even ordinary intelligent people of her court and surroundings – they didn't believe these incriminating documents were true. They could not possibly have done so. The letters and poems are full of the wildest contradictions. They are patched-up jobs, proving nothing. But in the Times of Mary Queen of Scots, legal truth quite obviously took on a political, not a moral significance. It was the truth of prop-aganda in aid of a cause that condemned Mary Queen of Scots. This is not to say she was guilty of the murder of her husband or otherwise. It is to say that there was no direct proof.'

Rowland, sleepily in the throes of his calming drug, kept his eyes on Chris, while Chris himself gazed with what looked like admiration at the lecturer throughout. Her voice was monotonous. She had the persevering tone of one who believed in and had thoroughly rehearsed what she was say-ing. Nina was anxious lest Rowland should really drop into sleep, which he barely avoided doing.

'... and,' proceeded Alice, 'another incidental point we can discern from the very casket letter we have been discussing: it was obviously the accepted mode of writing a long letter, to first make a list of the subjects to be covered, and then expand on the list. This remains to the present day a very good system. It was a system employed by the Queen, but the letter was grossly misrepresented by the list appearing in the text. But methodology aside, what is it that we find moved the sixteenth century political scene along life's way? What caused them to overlook plain facts in favour of propaganda? What caused the slaughter of Rizzio followed by the deliberate murder of Darnley? – Remember his house was not only blown up as he slept, but when he was found alive in the grounds he was actually slaughtered. The gunpowder was meant for him, not for the Queen. What was the cause? We are in the latter half of the sixteenth century, in Scotland. The causes of these homicides were jealousy, uncontrollable jealousy. And the subsequent execution of the Queen of Scots by the edict of Elizabeth? – It was hardly fear of treason. Mary was a prisoner. She could intrigue by word and pen, but she had no power. The secret, I feel, is jealousy. When James VI of Scotland, I of England, the son of Mary Queen of Scots was born, it is chronicled that Elizabeth exclaimed "The Queen of Scotland is delivered of a fair child and I am but barren stock." Jealousy, green jealousy, that was the motivation of the Age ...'

For the occasion, sherry was offered all round after the lecture. Chris had made a very graceful speech of thanks to Dr Barclay-Good on behalf of the school. She had, he said, widened and enlivened their awareness of the elements of hypocrisy prevalent in the society that had brought Mary Queen of Scots to judgment, a hypocrisy that serves its own ends, ignoring the simplest and most evident solutions such as the one he hoped to put forward in his forthcoming novel. Thank you, Dr Barclay-Good.

Alcoholic drinks were a great rarity at College Sunrise, unless smuggled in occasionally by the likes of Princess Tilly.

The sherry, as an event, was soon reflected in noisy chatter. The snacks were presided over by handsome young Albert who had attended the lecture, with a white apron tied over his gardening jeans. He himself took Coca-Cola.

Albert's only language was French and, perceiving both this, and his charming looks, Dr Alice engaged him in her best, not bad, conversational French. Rowland had disappeared.

As they went into dinner Nina put up an explanation for Rowland's absence. 'He was at the dentist this afternoon and had a heavy anaesthetic. I insisted he went to bed.'

'I noticed,' said Dr Alice blandly, 'that he was dopey.' She was under the impression he had slept through most of her lecture.

To Nina's rescue that evening, after dinner, came Israel Brown. He brought his very young aunt Giovanna with her violin, and, to everyone's rather stunned amazement, she played the solo theme of one of Niccolò Paganini's *capricci*.

'You know,' said Dr Alice, 'I was at a finishing school only a few miles from here. But it was very different from this. Much more strict.' She also said, 'Music speaks to you. It speaks.'

Giovanna smiled at her nephew and put away her lively violin.

It was raining heavily outside. Their guest was to leave early next morning for the airport. The party broke up at ten-thirty. Dr Alice was put in the attic guest-room. Nina said, 'I'm afraid you'll hear the rain thumping down on the roof.'

'Oh, I'm so tired, I'll sleep through everything.'

'It was a really wonderful talk,' said Nina. 'I can't tell you what it means to us. Chris was especially very enthralled, I could see. I only regret my husband was so much under the weather. But I know he'll want me to thank you again on his behalf.' The envelope containing the cheque for the fee and the fare had already been slipped into Dr Alice's hand. Nina was to take her guest to the airport immediately after breakfast. 'Good night. Good night.'

The house was silent already when, less than an hour later, Dr Alice was awakened by a tap on her door.

'Who's that?'

The door opened. She sat up in bed and switched on her bedside light.

Chris's red head appeared.

'May I have a word with you?'

'A word –'

'You're so magnificent,' he said. 'I just want to tell you that your insight into the life and times of Mary Queen of Scots, is simply astonishing. How could you divine so much? Jealousy. Enmity based on jealousy ...'

He came and sat on her bed.

'The hypocrisy of her accusers,' said Chris, '... the cynicism of it all. I was entranced to hear you speak. You looked so wonderful, and now, as you are, you look more stunning than I can say.'

'Look here,' she said.

But eventually, having discussed the era and circumstances of Mary Queen of Scots a little more, and after Chris had expanded on the subject of Dr Alice's splendid voice and appearance, he slid into bed with her. The rain danced on the roof. She was overcome by the redness of his hair and his young beauty, and succumbed with a faint cry.

Rowland was standing on the stairs leading down from the attic room when Chris let himself out. They did not exchange a word.

On the way to the airport in the morning Dr Alice said, 'Yours is a very advanced type of college.'

'Well, I hope it is,' said Nina.

'And the students very mature, I think.'

'They vary,' said Nina.

Rowland said later to Nina, 'Chris was in your scholar's room last night. He'll ruin the school. There won't be a next school year.'

'Get rid of him. Tell him to go,' Nina said.

'I can't.'

'Why not?'

'He needs me.'

'I know,' she said.

XIV

ROWLAND'S FATHER DIED. He flew to join his family in Yorkshire. He wrote to Chris:

> I fear there is a new book published a few months ago about Mary Queen of Scots and the murder of Darnley. By a scholar of the times. I advise you to read it and re-consider your thesis.

Chris sent an e-mail:

> I am a red-haired novelist of seventeen, soon to be world-famous as such. I weigh 160 lbs. I am at present 5' 10" still growing. Active sex life. Excellent health. I speak good French. I will successfully study Arabic and master German and Russian in the decades ahead. I will also continue to be a successful writer and first-class tennis player. Bury your dead.

Rowland e-mailed back:

> I have a degree in English and run a finishing school. I am 5' 11". I weigh 163 lbs. My French is excellent. My father was buried yesterday. – Rowland.

Chris took a print-out of the latter communication and pinned it to the school notice board where it was much admired until it was rescued and removed by Nina.

Rowland had intended to stay for a while with his family, his mother and aunt, both active middle-aged women, and a younger sister still at school. 'Stay for a while and relax,' Nina had exhorted him on the phone. But there arrived, daily, a local male health-counsellor to teach them how to grieve, so Rowland made off once more for Switzerland. He had been attached to his father, whose unexpected death had rather taken Rowland out of his problem with Chris. It was on the plane to Geneva that he started picking up the threads of his former obsession. He decidedly fought against the temptation to dwell on Chris, and longed for his more peaceful state of mind only the day before, when he had recalled his father in early days very dear to him, and was mourning him deeply. But the nearer he got to Geneva, the closer came Chris. No longer a boy-student, he was now a meaning, an explanation in himself.

Nina met him at the airport.

'I set a sort of exam,' she said. 'They wanted to sort of be reminded of what an exam was like. Do you know, our lot are remarkably clever.'

'Yes, they're all bright. What was the exam about?'

'What would you invest your money in, at a time of deep economic depression?'

'What did they say?'

Nina thought, He sounds bored, or am I imagining it?

She said, 'Tilly, if I remember, would buy a horse, maybe two, and rent them out as a reliable means of transport, and economical on the basis that oats are cheaper than petrol. Lionel would buy up all the automobile spare parts he could find, and lodge them in garages. This, on the reckoning that few people could afford new cars and would depend on repairs. Mary Foot, of course, has this fixation on pottery. For some reason she claims that rural ceramics would thrive in a depression. She spelt ceramics S-A-H-R-A-M-I-X. She really needs you, Rowland. She's left a letter for you condoling you on the death of your father. How are you feeling?'

'All right,' he said. 'I was all right yesterday and the day before, after the funeral. I was thinking of my father, thinking a lot about him. His death took Chris completely off my mind. But now, I can hardly wait till I get back into my brooding environment, if you know what I mean. I know I'm obsessed with Chris, but I want my obsession. So does he.'

'I think you're very bogged down.'

'It's his fault. Trying to pass himself off as a creative writer, when all he's doing is exploiting his looks and his youth.'

'It might be a thrilling book, all the same,' Nina said. 'Not historically sound, of course. But not impossible, just probable. Doesn't that fit in with what you always tell your class: You have to persuade the reader to read on?'

'My father's death made me forget him,' Rowland said.

'That's understandable.'

'Is it?'

'Yes. You have to see an analyst,' Nina said.

'I will if Chris will. The boy won't leave me alone.'

'Just hang on to the end of term,' Nina said. That, in fact, was what she was trying to do, herself. She said, 'Try to think about your father, about the times you spent with him.'

He said, 'My father's death was a respite.'

She thought: He needs a death. And not a word for me, not a look. No 'How are you feeling, I've missed you'. All I, I, I and 'my problem'. All I hope is that he doesn't murder Chris, that's all I care now.

Rowland said again, 'My father's death was a respite. Has Chris told you how much of his novel he still has to write?'

'No.'

'Have you seen any of it?'

'Only that bit at the beginning before you told him to give up the idea.'

'I shouldn't have said that. It made him cagey, secretive.'

'Well, I suppose so.'

Here they were at the gate of College Sunrise, Rowland thinking of the state of mind he had experienced on the death of his father, but unable to recapture it.

XV

THERE WAS A small sitting room at the back of College Sunrise, looking out on a leafy garden, which was generally used by the school's small staff, mainly Albert Hertz the lovely garden boy, Elaine Valette and her sister, Célestine, Chris's midnight lover. They met at tea and coffee breaks for a chat and a pause, and this afternoon they were joined by Claire Denis, the daily maid. Claire's apparently formidable task of cleaning and washing-up was considerably lightened by the appearance, once a month, of a house-cleaning team from Geneva, and the fact that the students were obliged to tidy up their rooms. Even so, Claire worked hard.

Their working hard was to-day partly the theme of the four who were gathered for tea and an understandable discussion of how they stood or would stand at College Sunrise when the new school year should begin in late January next. There was also the question of where the school would be located, since it was, by its foundation, free and mobile. Would their jobs be safe? Did they, individually, want the jobs to be safe?

As usual, the staff knew more about the crisis at the management end than Rowland and Nina or any of the students suspected.

Albert said, 'The lease runs out at the end of the year, but if they don't renew it someone else will take on the house. I like the garden, it's small but I've made it mine.'

'The marriage is finished,' said Célestine. 'Nina stays late with Israel Brown, and Rowland, wouldn't you know, is making for me. Would you believe it ... his jealousy of Chris. And he thinks I'll sleep with him instead of Chris, some hope.'

'Are you that fond of Chris?' said Claire.

'Oh yes, of course,' said Célestine, 'and he's got a great future. The publisher's arriving tomorrow. Rowland could kill him. I won't leave Rowland alone in my kitchen in case he puts poison in the food and kills us all to take Chris with us.'

'I wouldn't exaggerate,' said her sister. 'But I wonder what Chris will do when the school breaks up? You won't see him again.'

'I'd like a job in the hotel,' Célestine said.

'I'm thinking of a tourist bureau in Geneva,' said Elaine.

Claire said, 'I think of some sort of tragedy. Pallas's father has been arrested for smuggling a stolen picture. Israel's aunt Giovanna spotted it in a friend's gallery. They get to know everything in that world.'

Albert said, 'Nina's hoping the school's name will be famous through Chris's success. Put up the fees. But if it gets known about the picture ... a small El Greco, if it's real, worth fifteen.'

'Fifteen what?' said Claire.

'Million dollars.'

'But Chris,' said Célestine, 'helped Pallas to smuggle it out of Switzerland. It was in the hot-house with the tomatoes for a few weeks. Very bad for the paint.'

'And all the other students are so sweet,' said Elaine. 'I love Lionel, he's serious, Leg's fun, Tilly's rather a bitch but, well, she's Tilly. Lisa, Joan, Mary, especially Mary, who adores Rowland – they're charming. And Opal's going to be a woman priest, how long will that last?'

'Maybe I'll marry Opal,' said Albert. 'She grows on me.'

'The parents will be looking for a match, a *bon parti*.'

'I will marry her while the parents are still looking.' It was understood by all present that Albert had already made headway with Opal.

'I can always get a domestic job,' said Claire, 'but if Nina doesn't keep me on, I'll miss the school. – Albert, will you take your feet off the coffee table?'

'Will you travel?' said Célestine.

'Oh, yes.'

'Rowland won't go,' said Célestine. 'They are bound to part.'

The prospective publisher of Chris's novel checked in next day at the nearby hotel. Before Chris went to meet him he invited Rowland to accompany him.

'It would be nice, you know, if you represented the school as patron of the arts. You could let it be understood you were the mentor of the book.'

'Although I'm not,' said Rowland.

'Although you're not.'

'Go to hell.'

'Can I quote you, Rowland?'

'Whatever you please. It's hell you're going to, anyway.'

'I'm sorry to hear,' said Chris, 'that Célestine gave you the brush-off.'

'Did she?'

'I believe so, Rowland.'

'There may be another time,' Rowland said. 'Another occasion. Girls change their minds.'

'You'll come and meet my future publisher?'

'Do you have a contract already?'

'No. He's expressed an interest. That's sufficient.'

'All right. I'll come.'

Chris and Rowland were seated in one of the hotel's series of sitting rooms, one leading into another, each upholstered in a different floral pattern. Nina had offered the hospitality of the school but Chris had said he preferred to be independent.

It was four-thirty in the afternoon, the time of their appointment with Monty Fergusson the London publisher who had checked into the hotel at about two o'clock. Rowland left a message at the desk for the publisher, telling him where to find them.

A clerk from the desk approached them: 'Mr Wiley?'

'That's me,' said Chris.

'A message from Mr Fergusson. He sent down a message to say he's detained with some business on the phone to London and will be half-an-hour late. Can he offer you something to drink while waiting or would you prefer to return later?'

Rowland said, 'Well, I –'

'We'll wait,' said Chris.

Rowland ordered a single malt, Chris, a Coca-Cola.

'Has he read your book, so far as it goes?' Rowland said.

'I expect so.'

'Perhaps he's actually looking at it now. Those big firms employ readers. The publishers don't read everything themselves.'

'Mine is a special case.'

'Yes,' said Rowland.

'Can you ever get me out of your mind?'

'You're not on my mind. In fact, all the time I was in Yorkshire I didn't give you a thought.'

Their drinks arrived.

'Perhaps we should pay,' said Chris.

'Certainly not. Why have you suddenly lost your confidence?'

'Oh, fame's a new experience for me. I'll get used to it. Your father's death made you forget me.'

'Oh, yes.'

'Maybe you need another death to get over your obsession. A more important one.'

'Let's hope not,' said Rowland.

The windows of the room looked over the steel-grey lake. The surface was rough, the sky over-clouded. None the less, it was a handsome scene. Rowland was impatient for the publisher to arrive and enjoy the fine scene while it was still daylight. He said, 'Once the school breaks up and you go away, you know I'm going to reorganize my life. I want you to leave me alone, though.' It was evident that he spoke as if he had a choking sensation, which in fact he had.

'You will not murder me,' said Chris.

Rowland sipped his drink and gazed out of the window. Chris said, 'You will murder Nina.'

'What?'

'Nina. The papers will say you found her in bed with her lover. *Crime passionnel.* Something you'd have to live with, and forget me. A death.'

'You're mad, more mad than me,' said Rowland.

'And it will be bad for the school,' Chris said.

A very tall figure was approaching their table. Monty Fergusson, about fifty, with a shock of white hair surrounding a smooth, youngish face.

'Nice place,' he said, meaning who knows what?

'I'm Rowland Mahler,' said Rowland. 'This is Chris.'

Monty Fergusson took Rowland's hand, and nodded to Chris. He had been put on the plane for Geneva that morning with a bulky piece of manuscript to read: The famous novel or rather, book, by the sort of famous youngster of seventeen. The boy had been well photographed and talked about. There would probably be a film. Monty was given to understand that the book involved 'a new theory of the murder of Mary

Queen of Scots' husband.' A good commercial proposition
while it lasted. Monty had started to look through it on the
plane, flicking over the pages so as to absorb the paragraphs
here and there, and for the last twenty-five minutes up in his
room he had read the opening chapters entirely, and the last
ten pages of the unfinished script.

'Our school,' said Rowland, 'also looks over the lake.'

Monty sat with the fat package on his lap and looked at
Chris. 'You've put in a lot of work, here.'

'Oh, yes, I should be finished quite soon. I have two alternative endings. I have to make a choice.'

'Yes, choice ... Choices are rather a problem aren't they?'

'It will turn out all right.'

'It will be all right because of your youth and the public-
ity you've spread about. How far has the film project come
along? Do you have a contract?'

'Not yet. Of course, they're waiting for publication of the
book itself.'

'The book itself,' said the publisher, 'is actually a lot of shit.'

'Oh, come,' said Rowland in a very soft, awed, voice.

'Are you trying to beat down the price?' said Chris.

'I haven't made an offer,' said the publisher.

'But there are other publishers, other offers,' said Chris.

'And other authors,' said Monty. 'Which reminds me I
have to hire a car to get back to Geneva for dinner tonight.
I have an author to see, there in Geneva. Very interesting ...'
He got up and went to the desk to order his car. When he
came back he didn't sit down again. He merely shook their
hands and said to Chris, 'I'll be interested to see the final
draft. Our readers will get copies. I think, though, you'll have
a lot of work to do on the book. That would be up to the
editors if they could re-work it. If they could ... Nice to see
you. Goodbye. Goodbye.'

XVI

THAT CHRIS'S BOOK needed a whole lot of work on it was a story that soon caught on in the swift tale-bearing publishing world. Chris, struggling with his alternative endings, was now stuck in his final chapter. Shaken by Monty Fergusson's reaction he telephoned a literary agent, from whose tone he sensed a decided drop in enthusiasm for his forthcoming novel.

'Monty Fergusson is an enemy,' he told Nina, who reported it to Rowland.

'Not an enemy of yours, anyway,' Rowland said. He didn't go so far as to tell her that Chris could be regarded as her enemy, but he recounted calmly the embarrassing encounter in the hotel sitting room with Monty Fergusson.

'He's reputed to be tough,' Nina said.

'Where money's concerned they're all tough. It's only because he's a juvenile prodigy that Chris has all this attention. Perhaps if he was an active author of 100 years old in a wheel-chair the result would be the same.'

'But he looks nice and wild. The younger set will like him.'

'The younger people don't read books much. They're not all like us.'

'What about the movie?'

'If you ask me,' said Rowland, shaking a lock of hair off his face, 'the whole thing's an air-bubble. The book's a lot of shit.'

'That isn't unusual.'

'No, it isn't.'

She could see Rowland was less tense, even pleased at the awful meeting with the very busy publisher. She noticed he was making notes on his computer. He looked up and said, 'Practical jokers can easily become psychopaths, don't you think?'

'Oh, yes, but what has Chris actually done that's awful?' said Nina.

'He has awful ideas.'

'Oh, ideas ...'

Tilly was all-vigilant. She made it her business to know that a few days later Chris had put through a call to an alternative publisher, who was expected to ring him back but didn't.

She went to see him in his room. 'There's no need to panic,' she told him.

'Perhaps not for me,' said Chris.

Fax to Alexander Archer:

Dear Dad,

I'm glad to hear you got promotion, you are going to need the money there is this dance coming up at the end of term one of us outshining the other a five star do, and there is a boutique in Lausanne with some dresses of my choice. My shoes are worn down like a tramp and I need levis and warm tops you wouldnt let me freeze Get the message in detail just send me the money. Your coming to the dance bring Melinda for my choice. We can go on to Rome or Paris for Xmas and N. Year what a good idea before going home, to soften the blow. Pallas Kapelases father George has been arrested in Germany for smuggling a stolen painting not el Greco but a school of. It's all a cooked up plot because Mr Kapelas is a spy and they know it. But Nina's lover Israel Brown the Art gallerist knows all about it and says confidentially which is why Im telling you that Kapelas is mixed up with everything and the only solution for him is religion, he should go to a monastery. In spite of all that Israel is in love with Nina and pulling the strings to get Pallases Dad released if only on bail, then he can always get away. Rowland's father died we held a prayer meeting for him. Now R. has got his inspiration back. A publisher came to Ouchy about Chris's Novel sight unseen but he read it on the way and by the time he got to his hotel he regretted it and gave Chris a bad time which gave Rowland a good time as I told you that's the way it goes and we don't know what to think. He (Rowland) goes on with our English classes I bet you don't know what a gerund is, also our creative writing class which I love. Chris keeps away, hes more like a lodger than a student. Of course hes very close to Pallas. Something is going on between them, not sex as Pallas says she has to be a virgin when she marries. But she looks after his private papers and scripts I still think he is a genius and hope he won't commit suicide. Im counting the days don't forget my cash love and kisses Joan

Giovanna Brown arrived in Lausanne to join her nephew at Ouchy for a long weekend. She found him absorbed with Nina. She was in the way even though the house was a big one. The Browns knew few people in those parts and it seemed that all of those few were away in London, in the West Indies, New York, anywhere but in already cold Ouchy.

'Where is that red-haired genius I played my violin to?' she said to Nina, who was about to have lunch in the kitchen with Israel.

'He's at the school. Rather depressed. His publisher-to-be didn't rave over the book.'

'Has he written a book, then?'

'Almost,' said Nina.

Giovanna found a plastic shopping bag and put in it some fruit juice, a tin of pâté and some biscuits. With this, she set off for the school on Israel's motor-bike.

The school were at lunch. Giovanna put her head round the door of the dining-room. Rowland stood up: 'Anything wrong? Nina –'

'Nina is lunching with Israel.'

'Well, I know that.'

'I've come for Chris. I've brought a picnic.'

'No need for that. Sit down. Célestine will get you a plate.' He waved a hand towards her, 'You've all met Giovanna.'

There was a vacant chair beside Lionel, opposite Chris. She sat there, and when her place was laid she helped herself to some salad-like mixture out of a very large bowl.

'You want to see me?' Chris said.

'What are you up to?' Giovanna said.

'But you, what are you up to?' said Chris. 'Shouldn't you be at your music school?'

'I flew in from Vienna for the weekend to see Isy. He's utterly engaged, so here I am. Amuse me.'

'Read some of your book to Giovanna,' said Tilly.

'All right. You can all listen,' said Chris.

'We have a poetry class this afternoon,' said Rowland, 'followed by a special lecture by our neighbour and Giovanna's nephew Israel Brown on the modern Irish movement in art.'

The students then fell to investigating the strange nature of young Giovanna's relationship to Israel the elder, which she elaborately explained. Chris arranged with Giovanna to see her after lunch, promising to read her some of his book.

She joined him in front of the fire in the school sitting-room. He hadn't brought his book, but he outlined it to her up to the point he had reached.

'Does it sound like a lot of shit?' he said.

'Oh no, it sounds a perfectly good story. This Queen hates her beastly husband and loves the charming little Italian musician who makes her so happy. The husband gets terribly jealous and gangs up with his friends to kill the sweet musician, so the musician's young brother gangs up with his influential friends abroad and brings them to kill that husband of the Queen. It's a great story. There's an opera on those same lines by Donizetti. The Queen of Scotland calls the Queen of England "Vile Bastard". It's great. What's your problem?'

'The publisher thinks the young brother couldn't possibly be involved. But anyway, it's a work of fiction. Novelists can say what they like. I only have a problem with the ending. There are two alternative endings. One, we see the Queen late in life before her execution –'

'Was she put to death?'

'Oh yes. She plotted against the Queen of England.'

'Yes, now I remember that in the opera.'

'Anyway, here she is reflecting on her past life and the whole affair. I don't know for sure if Rizzio the musician was her lover, by the way. She was so tall and he was so tiny.'

'It could be an attraction of opposites,' said Giovanna.

'Does that often happen?' Chris said.

'It happens all the time.'

'Well, I'll think of that for my second draft. The second alternative ending is this. We see Rizzio's brother Jacopo, who I make a musician, too, received in honour by his family in Italy. He is given a public welcome by the town, having vindicated his brother's death. I haven't decided which ending to close my novel with.'

'Do both,' said Giovanna. 'First, the Queen looking back on her love-life full of the language of music, and second, the hero's welcome.'

'Well,' said Chris, 'I'll think of that, too. It does me good to talk to you. I'm hoping for a movie, you know.'

'For a movie,' she said, 'I'd put the young brother's home-coming first with his playing some photogenic instrument. Then I'd put the Queen looking back on the romantic life as she walks to her death.'

XVII

ELAINE VALETTE, French teacher and secretary, had tolerated her younger sister Célestine's affair with Chris, but was decidedly opposed to Rowland's efforts to seduce the girl. She felt, anyway, that he was not so interested in Célestine as he was in rivalling Chris. She took ground from her professional arrangement with the school, and said she found she could not do two jobs: look after the office and teach.

Nina, to whom she had made her protest, pointed out that she and Rowland each did at least three jobs. In fact, Nina took a class in meteorology (which was very popular, especially with aspiring weather forecasters), and a 'business' class, which included her '*comme il faut*' sessions; she also kept in touch with the parents. Rowland, she pointed out, taught literature, art and various subjects besides helping to run the school.

But Elaine was adamant. Nina sensed something in the girl's tone that sounded like a heavy moral judgment. There were not a great many weeks to the end of their school year, and so Nina was not unduly worried; she was only tired, already, at the thought of so much office labour to come, without Elaine's help. But, in addition, she felt this other sensation of some moral objection.

'Is Chris bothering your sister?' Nina said.

'No, it's Rowland. Can you blame him?'

'Yes, of course I can.'

'How can you blame him when you spend your spare energy with Mr Brown?'

Energie ... The word in French made Nina laugh aloud. She said, 'Where I go outside the school is entirely my business. If Rowland's troubling you or your sister in the school I'll give him hell.'

The girl left haughtily.

'You've upset Elaine,' Nina said when she saw Rowland.

'Elaine?'

'Yes, Elaine. Célestine's sister,' Nina said.

'How absurd. What's upset her?'

'Apparently you are pursuing Célestine.'

'As things stand ... Well, I don't think you can complain.'

'Elaine won't do any more office work. Who's going to take on her office job?'

'Me. I'll do it if she doesn't change her mind as she probably will, tomorrow. In any case I intend to keep on College Sunrise in the new year. I'll move somewhere else. I don't know what you intend to do, Nina.'

She didn't reply, not knowing, in fact, what she intended to do. She knew that her love affair with Israel Brown was not a secret, but the happiness of her love sustained her as if a secret was shared; to talk of it now would be to break a spell. She was afraid that Rowland would appeal to her, the marriage, the partnership, the school, his need to write a novel or something.

Nina had sometimes wondered if Elaine was attracted to Rowland, or even if there was something between them. She had never thought of Célestine in connection with Rowland, and now she began to reflect that, after all, Célestine was Chris's girl, and so Rowland continued to have Chris predominantly in mind.

She felt they had said enough for the time being. She left, got in the car and went to the hairdresser from where she phoned her lover.

'Rowland's wearing an earring to-day,' she said.

'Perhaps he just forgot to take it off.'

'Are you serious about Nina?' Giovanna said to Israel.

'Yes, altogether serious. She's wonderful.'

'And the husband?'

'I think his problem is spiritual.'

'You say that about everybody. You said it once about me.'

'Did I? Perhaps I was right.'

'No, my problems are musical.'

She got into her car and left for the airport.

So much for the red-haired genius, thought Israel.

And he pondered ahead, that the school would probably continue one more year at Ouchy and that, aged eighteen, Chris might join Rowland in another city, perhaps Rome, as a business partner in College Sunrise, specializing in creative writing, and that they would in fact live together.

It was only a speculation. Israel Brown did not take into account the eventual flamboyant literary success of Chris himself, if not entirely of his book, so that he would immediately set himself to write another. But Israel's general prediction was near enough: Rowland would not seek to keep Nina. Her absence, like his father's death, would bring him peace of mind.

Rowland proceeded fiercely, now, with his Book of Observations. Nina read his latest handwritten entry:

A perfect marriage, one partner of which is a great and successful artist, probably can exist, but very, very rarely. The difficulty lies in conflicting dedications. Most marriages, where both or one is an artist, are rickety. – Most marriages of this kind comprise one failed artist.

The dedication of an artist involves willing oblivion to everything else while the art is being practised, and for the hours antiguous to it.

Nina looked up 'antiguous' in the dictionary but couldn't find it. She changed it to 'contiguous'. Then she wrote, on the next line: 'Tilly is pregnant by Albert.'

Princess Tilly, as she styled herself, apparently with some inherited right, had fallen out with her family on grounds of imputed activities unbefitting her one-time royal connections. No-one seemed to know who they were, but in fact they existed in a remote estate in a mountainous republic in Eastern Europe.

'It's so near the end of term, her pregnancy won't be noticed at the dance,' Nina said to Israel Brown. 'Albert the gardener is perhaps more of a difficulty.'

'Oh, quite. The poorer people are always affected by illegitimacy. People like Tilly don't need to worry. Her type of family can always absorb an infant. But the young man – does he want to be a father?'

'Oh, yes, that's the problem. He wants to marry her. Last week he wanted to marry Opal Gross but now he wants Tilly.'

'The family will never allow it.'

'No. And she herself doesn't want to marry him. She's going to have the baby, all the same.'

'It's a religious problem, fundamentally.'

'I knew you'd say that,' Nina said. 'If you mean just being fair, she's much too young for marriage, but I think she should give Albert access to the baby when it's born.'

'No doubt she would be obliged to do that if it came to a court order.'

'Oh, my God. Court order … could we be sued for lack of vigilance, or something? – Tilly's only seventeen and a half.'

'Yes, I suppose you could be sued, but you won't be.'

'She's making no secret of it,' Nina said. 'The school's all excited.'

'She has good taste. Your gardener's good-looking.'

XVIII

CHRIS HAD two more publishers on his immediate list. When he had swallowed the shock of Monty Fergusson's remarks he wrote to both of them to say his book was nearing completion. Their replies reflected separately the extent to which Monty's reaction had or had not probably reached them. One of the publishers, a woman, was effusive as ever. The other, a man, had turned cool. Chris persuaded Nina to let him invite the woman publisher to see him, and put her up in College Sunrise's attic bedroom. And by the following week, on the notice board of the school appeared an apparent newspaper diary cutting describing the untimely death of Monty Fergusson, publisher (51) due to a heart-attack brought on by the excitement of shooting a squirrel on the lawn. As everyone in the school had now heard Monty's name, Chris was able to put about with some plausibility that he had put the evil eye on the publisher. Rowland took down the notice and, at dinner, informed the school that Chris had got a local printer to produce the paragraph. Was it amusing?

'No,' said Lionel. 'It's childish.'

'It could still be amusing,' said Chris.

'What's funny about it?' said Mary Foot.

'The death of that man would always be funny,' Chris said.

'I suppose he's entitled to his opinion,' said Nina.

'And I to wish him death,' said Chris.

'I think,' said Rowland, 'I'd feel the same. After all, I know … I was there.'

'Let's hope the new one is better. Has she read any of your book?' Nina said.

'She'll be reading it soon. I sent it by express.'

'Good luck, Chris,' said Nina.

'Good luck,' said everybody.

Grace Formby, the publisher, arrived the following week, tall, thin, well over forty and at the same time well under fifty, and in fact she would have been and would be, forty-five for many years. She had long fingers with a lot of rings on both hands, and a few chains hanging from her neck and some bracelets. She clinked as she approached, having been relieved of her coat. Rowland had collected her at the airport and had brought her to the study to meet Nina and Chris for a private preliminary drink.

'Chris,' she said, 'I've been up all night reading your novel. It's great. Of course we'll have to do some editing. I think as you say you should end it with both your endings, and the Queen going to the scaffold.'

'The block,' Chris said.

'The block. You know there are so many books and plays about Mary Queen of Scots. Never a year passes –'

'And Bonivard?' said Chris.

'Bonivard?'

'He's the Genevan hero who was imprisoned in the Castle of Chillon. It's near here. You know Byron's poem –'

'Oh yes, of course. It's a romantic place, here. Lovely view. Just right for a novel. I'm always casing for novels wherever I rove. This would be an ideal setting. I'd love to see over your school.'

'As a matter of fact,' Rowland said, 'I'm writing a book about this place just at the moment. It's provisionally called *Observations*. It's about our school here at Ouchy.'

'I'm in editorial mode,' she said.

The upshot of the visit was a close friendship struck between Rowland and Grace Formby which was to lead to her firm's publication of his book *The School Observed*. This incipient friendship was obvious to Chris all through the publisher's stay. She came down to dinner even more bejezebelled around her neck and wrists, and fairly engulfed Rowland with her enthusiasm. In compensation, she told Chris she had brought with her a draft contract which he could read at leisure. But his satisfaction was dismissed by her saying that perhaps a historian should be consulted about the actual mechanics of the murder.

'Which murder?' demanded Chris, who suspected she hadn't read his book very thoroughly.

'Well, the fifty-six stab wounds,' said Grace.

'That's the murder of Rizzio, not Darnley.'

'Well, I only say a history scholar will have to read it. No doubt we can make any necessary adjustments, Chris. Nobody expects you to know everything at your age. Some of the TV questioners can be tough, but you'll certainly carry it off.' She added in a high, thin voice: 'Great hair. Is that it's natural colour?'

Rowland and Chris took Grace Formby to the airport the next morning. On the way back Rowland said to Chris, 'If I were in your place I'd sign that contract before they change their minds.'

'It will be gone through with a tooth-comb,' said Chris. 'My family has company lawyers stationed at every whistle-stop. We never read our own contracts. They do.'

'Then you might easily lose this one,' Rowland said. 'It's so true that Mary Queen of Scots is very much written about. Everywhere you look is Mary Queen of Scots.'

'Which reflects public interest,' said Chris.

'I would be cautious,' said Rowland, 'of a subject so very much worked on.'

'I have a unique, original theory,' Chris said. 'And look, Rowland, I can see very well that you're trying to exploit my talent and my contacts to further your own literary ambitions.'

'I should have thought that it was you who are exploiting my hospitality and my school to further your literary ambitions.'

'I pay.'

'You can get out.'

'Too simple. You have to wait till the end of term. It won't be long. If you want to survive to that date just keep your hands off my publisher.'

'You need therapy, Chris.'

They were nearly home, and they drove on in a silence broken only once by a burst of unnecessary laughter from Chris.

Only Mary Foot and Joan Archer were to return to the school in the New Year for another term. Nina had enrolled six new students and arranged for a further year's lease of the Ouchy premises. She had laid all this before Rowland who had accepted the situation passively. He knew that Nina would not be there. He could hardly grasp the fact that he was still married to Nina. Their separation had not been planned; it had just come about.

Nina now even confided in the students how she would go to join Israel Brown at his wonderful art gallery, a totally new life. She would study modern art. After the December dance the school would break up. Rowland would then take over College Sunrise.

'I won't be here,' Tilly said.

'You should go home to your family. I'll write a letter,' Nina said.

'No, I've got a job through a friend in Frankfurt. I'm to be a photographic model for maternity clothes at all stages.'

'And Albert?' said Joan Archer. She was anxious for something new to write to her father.

'He could also be a photo model,' said Tilly. 'But he likes his gardening better. Opal is furious that he wants to marry me, but I won't think of it.'

'You're much too young to think of it,' said Nina.

Everyone agreed with that.

Nina proceeded with her *comme il faut* class which was to the effect that no-one benefited from smoking pot. 'The air was thick with smoke when I went up to the second floor the other day. Claire has complained that it gets on her chest. You just have to realize that the more you smoke the less you appreciate it, and you go on to stronger things. It's up to you because you're leaving soon and you can do what you like or whatever you can get away with. But Rowland has said I can tell you about his brother, who went from pot to the hard stuff. He robbed to get the drug and he folded up and died aged nineteen. Rowland's father, who died recently, never got over it.'

Everyone had a story to tell, how they had heard of the drastic results of drug-fancying, soft and hard. Nina knew that most of them, however, had at some time managed to obtain and smoke the stuff. She added, 'It's like smoking cigarettes in one respect, it's dreadfully low, it's common.'

This dubious proposition seemed to have a generally awesome effect on most of Nina's students which lasted till teatime. Lionel Haas was an exception.

'A great many top people take cocaine and smoke cigarettes,' he said.

'Who are they?'

He had nobody on the tip of his tongue, so Nina rapidly closed the session.

It was Rowland's creative writing class which he sometimes, like to-day, worked in with a poetry session. He had prepared a short lecture which he read from his Book of Observations:

'Art is an act of daring,' said Rowland.

'A marriage that can survive the ruthlessness of art is one of sacrifice on the part of the non-artist partner. If both practise the same art you should know that one of them will invariably be inferior to the other.

'If, in the course of an author's preparing a book, his family suffers a blow or a tragedy, the book could easily come to ruin in the ensuing domestic anguish and muddle. The average author can no doubt finish the book, but not well. However the dedicated author might seem callous, not easily shattered, tough. Hence the reputation of artists in all fields for ruthless, cold detachment. Too bad. About this sort of accusation the true artist is uncaring. The true artist is almost unaware of other people's cares and distractions. This applies to either sex.

'Once you have written The End to a book it is yours, not only till death do you part but for all eternity. Translators and adaptors come and go, but they can't lay claim to the authorship of a work that is yours. Remember this if you ever take up the literary profession, as you all seem very keen to do.

'A lot of talk goes on about ideas. I heard a popular singer at an arts festival giving vent to his ideas about ideas. What was wanted, he said, were ideas, not just skill with words. Now, I challenge you to express any idea adequately without skill with words. Words are ideas. That great Gospel according to St John opens: "In the beginning was the Word."'

Rowland then read a poem that the class was to study for his next lesson. 'Page 738 of your book,' he said. 'Thomas Hardy 1840–1928, his poem *In Tenebris*, meaning in the shadows. A man is in mourning for his loved one. It is about the experience of separation.

> Wintertime nighs;
> But my bereavement-pain
> It cannot bring again:
> Twice no one dies.
>
> Flower-petals flee;
> But, since it once hath been,
> No more that severing scene
> Can harrow me.
>
> Birds faint in dread:
> I shall not lose old strength
> In the lone frost's black length:
> Strength long since fled!
>
> Leaves freeze to dun;
> But friends can not turn cold
> This season as of old
> For him with none.
>
> Tempests may scath;
> But love can not make smart
> Again this year his heart
> Who no heart hath.

Black is night's cope;
But death will not appal
One who, past doubtings all,
Waits in unhope.

Mary Foot was crying. 'Oh, how sad everything is,' she said. 'And just at the end of the term ...'

'It's not our sadness, Mary,' said Rowland. 'It was Thomas Hardy's. What I want you all to do for Thursday afternoon next, is to give me your thoughts on verse 3, line 1. 'Birds faint in dread.' What did Hardy mean? Do birds ever faint? And do they faint in fear? Hardy was a countryman. Perhaps he knew the answer. A strange line. See what you make of it. Cheer up, Mary my dear.'

In fact, on Thursday, Rowland was to be prevented from taking his class, and so the question of the fainting bird was never resolved.

XIX

IT WAS THURSDAY morning, the day of Rowland's scheduled creative writing class. It would be the last of the term. The school broke up at the end of the week, after the dance on Saturday night.

Rowland, as he lay in his bath, remembered, too, that he had arranged to play Lionel Haas at squash in the neighbouring hotel.

The bathroom adjacent to Rowland and Nina's bedroom, was a cold one. The central-heating radiator hardly worked but they had put in a small electric heater which Nina had already turned on, having had her bath earlier.

Suddenly the bathroom door opened. Rowland looked round for Nina but found Chris in his pyjamas, standing in the doorway.

'What are you doing here?' Rowland said.

'You've been in touch with my publisher, Grace Formby. I've been thinking it over. You're going to use me as a rung in your ladder,' Chris said.

'Don't be absurd. Get out of here.'

'And write a book about living with adolescents and teenagers, the only thing you know.'

'Get out of my bathroom,' Rowland said. He sat up and reached for his long-handled bath-brush, and started scrubbing his back.

'I heard from Grace Formby. She has confirmed my contract,' Chris said.

'Very good. I'm glad. Congratulations.'

'You have exploited me,' said Chris.

There was a rapid movement. Chris's bright red head bent suddenly before Rowland's eyes. If what happened in the next part-second could be described in slow motion it was this: Chris bent down and grabbed the little live heater in both hands, holding it high above his head. He approached the bath. 'You'll kill me. Put that down,' yelled Rowland. Exactly as he spoke he jabbed Chris in the groin with his bath-brush and vaulted over the bath. At the same instant, Chris, in pain from the jab bent forward so that the live electric stove fell into the water. The lights went out, as it was discovered later all over the house. Rowland felt a quiver up his leg. His heel had been seared. The water still sizzled with the heat of the fire, where Rowland was so very nearly electrocuted.

Chris disappeared.

'This *would* happen to-day when I'm busy about the dance,' Nina said when she was trying to obtain one electrician after another on the phone. She had imagined that the electricity failure was a normal breakdown.

Rowland limped in to the office with his burnt foot, in a shocked condition. He was dripping wet. 'What's happened?' he said, so foolishly that she knew something had gone wrong. 'Chris,' she thought.

She wanted to hand Chris over to the police. She found him in his room, fully dressed and writing at his desk.

'I'm going to denounce you to the police for attempted murder.'

'And how will you explain my presence in Rowland's bathroom?'

'How will I explain … ?'

'Oh, yes. I'm a minor. Do you want Rowland to keep on the school? Better not get him a bad name.'

'Rowland's foot was burnt by the fire,' she said.

'Then he can't dance.'

Rowland could not dance but he went to the party all the same. It was a considerable success. All the students seemed to be related to, or friends with, so many prosperous people that sixty tickets were easily sold. Chris attended, with his mother and uncle.

Nina said to the uncle, 'I hope you are going to take Chris back with you.'

'I was afraid you'd say that,' said the uncle.

And, when supper was served, Nina found herself near Chris's mild-looking mother. 'I hope you are going to take Chris back with you.'

'What is your problem?' said the woman, fiercely.

'We don't want him.'

'Chris is talented and you are all jealous. Especially your husband. So many people are jealous of Chris.'

Someone at the table, whose order had not yet arrived, said, 'I think "waiter" is such a funny word. It is we who wait.'

Rowland was to continue to run College Sunrise with some success.

After another year at Ouchy he moved to Ravenna where the school specialized in the study of mosaics. From there he moved to Istanbul where he met with many problems too complicated to narrate here. His book, *The School Observed*, was published satisfactorily, as was Chris's first novel, highly praised for its fine, youthful disregard of dry historical facts.

Chris proceeded to establish himself as a readable novelist and meanwhile joined Rowland at College Sunrise as soon as he was of age. After a year they engaged themselves in a Same-sex Affirmation Ceremony, attended by friends and Chris's family.

Nina settled in London, married to Israel Brown and happy with her studies and his gallery. She returned with him to his villa at Ouchy from time to time. The house of College Sunrise was now a youth hostel. When she passed the house, she sometimes felt nostalgia, not at all for Rowland, but for College Sunrise itself.

Pallas Kapelas – her father had skipped bail, was wanted and always would be. Pallas married a merchant shipowner and was, so far, contented.

Nina had not heard from Lionel Haas, not a word.

Pansy Leghorn had a temporary job as an editor at the BBC.

Princess Tilly had a baby girl who, as Israel Brown had predicted, was nursed and coddled into Tilly's family, while Tilly went her own way and became a society journalist. Albert visited his daughter from time to time, taking her a teddy bear and a bedside clock.

Opal Gross was in the process of studying for the Anglican ministry.

Mary Foot opened a shop in Cornwall where she sold ceramics and transparent scarves. She corresponded regularly with Rowland and Chris, passing on their news to Nina.

Lisa Orlando got a place at Southampton University, reading psychology.

Joan Archer got a place in a good drama school, as she had for so long desired. Eventually, she was to write television scripts.

Albert was kept on at the house as a gardener, and Claire as a domestic helper.

Elaine got a job in Geneva at a travel agency. She frequently met Albert at weekends and public holidays.

Her sister, Célestine, had a job at the restaurant of a skating rink in Lausanne, where she also progressed wonderfully at skating.

Nina, now finding herself obliged to give dinner parties at Ouchy for the sophisticated world of art-dealers, would arrange with the hotel to provide the catering. And once, on her way to the hotel on just such an errand, on a summer evening, she heard once more from the open windows, the chatter of young voices, so that it seemed almost like College Sunrise again. She waved to Albert. And she heard the dear voice of Hazel forecasting the weather on Sky News: 'As we go through this evening and into tonight ...'